Horse, I Am Your Mother:

Stories by Ron Vossler

The Simon Johnson Guild, Inc.
Fargo

Library of Congress Catalog Card Number 88-82754

ISBN 0-9621903-0-6

Illustrated by Trygve Olson

Designed by Sue Poitras

First Edition

2

To all my relatives who are scattered, as my dad would say, from heck to breakfast: the Boschees, Woehls, Fetzers, Delzers, and Vosslers--this collection is dedicated.

This project was funded by the
North Dakota Centennial Commission

Our Fathers finde their graves in our short memories

--Sir Thomas Browne

Horse, I Am Your Mother

Table of Contents

Friederich The Wild and The Defense Of Fort Schuffnudala

My great-grandmother Phillibina was elbow deep in dough when Friederich the Wild, my great-grandfather, who'd heard the news from a neighbor, burst through the door of their semeljank, or sodhouse, on their homestead in Dakota Territory and shouted, "Die Indianer kommt," or, for those of you who don't view the world through the bifocals of our language, "The Indians are coming."

Phillibina threw the dough into a pillow case, and much to the delight of their four year old son Fortunato, my larval grandfather, who was already an habitual "suessgusch," or, as you'd say in English, a sweetmouth (and who was already known as Slavak, which means slave or sloppy)--I say, much to little Slavak's delight, Phillibina spread a swath of chokecherry jelly over his face with the dim hope that should she and Friederich be massacred by the Indians rumoured to have left their reservation, her little son might be spared, mistaken for one of the renegades' own kind.

Friederich was no stranger to combat. As a draftee from German colonies on the Black Sea, he had once been in the Russian cavalry and he wanted to fight it out on the spot. But Phillibina, pointing her dough-covered finger in the direction of New Odessa, the nearest settlement twelve miles to the east, summed up the entire situation in one of her pithy proverbs, and determined their course of action, by saying, "Death is free, but it costs you your life."

Assuming the worst, they hurriedly loaded their wagon with everything they felt unable to leave behind, for only the Lord knew if they'd ever return. Phillibina wrapped her little jelly-face in her dearest belonging, a many-hued tuechle shawl her mother had knitted in the old country, while Friederich grabbed his astrakhan greatcoat, not so much for the coat, which was threadbare and well-ventilated from Turkish gunfire, but for his prized possession he kept in a small tobacco bag tucked deep in its pocket: a piece of white cake, dried and crumbling now, that he'd received as a gift from the hand of the Queen Mother of all the Russias herself, when as a member of the Czar's bodyguard he'd retrieved her ivory comb from the mud outside her private rail car on the way to Tsarskoe Seloe. As for Slavak, he took his favorite plaything, in fact his only plaything, something he'd salvaged from butchering day, a severed chicken foot he called "chicken snitcher," for by pulling on a tendon at the joint he could make the claws close into a tight grip. (It had already been tested in combat, used as an extension of his own arm to reach under laying hens that pecked, when it was time for him to gather eggs.)

So while our little family makes their way towards town, their wagon pulled by two plodding oxen, and while little Slavak licks cheek-to-cheek on our well-jostled Phillibina's lap, and while Friederich sets his lantern jaw into the wind and like some Queeg of the prairies reaches into his pocket and fondles his keep-sake, remembering long white fingers and less fear-ful times--while all this is happening, let me tell you about my great-aunt Sophie, or as we called her in our system of reckoning, Sophie-Bass.

At the time of our story she hadn't been born yet. She was still dutifully coiled in Phillibina's embryonic fluids, adrift on her own private sea, on her own nine-month voyage to a new world, emigrating if you want to call it that. But her condition then would never deter her from recounting that awful ride to escape the Indians. Over the course of almost the next cen-tury, at reunions and church picnics and funerals, whenever anyone would listen and even when they wouldn't, Sophie "The Endless," as she came to be known, would tell about every bump and rock on that journey, complain about the buffalo wallow halfway to town that rattled her gums, vent her most vehe-ment criticism on the glacier that during the last ice age had not picked up after itself like a good German, leaving the prairie covered with stones, and blame her arthritic fingers on the grip she had to assume then, saying, "You try holding on for twelve miles sometimes."

While they are heading to town, we can spare ourselves the jolting ride while I assail you with a lit-tle information about Friederich. No, I am not going to compose a paean of the American dream and how it once had blown sweet relief of freedom though the steppe-like recesses of Friederich's mind, for his first years in Dakota Territory were not easy ones. He slept badly, despite the fact that he worked long and hard. At night in his sodhouse, with Phillibina beside him plunged as deep in sleep as she usually was in bread dough, Friederich lay with his eyes open, or as he put it later, "Drilling holes into the dark." (And if we lean on Sophie-Bass's version of that time, for she was an avid gardener in her later years, we find her saying, "Yah, Papa always shook at night, like my hollyhocks in a high wind.") In the cries of the wolves, ducks or geese, Friederich thought he discerned the signals of Russian agents creeping up on him. During the day, when he was plowing, he anxiously scanned the horizon for signs of visitors, and if he saw anyone he ran for his shotgun. In town, in every face he saw the possibility of an enemy, and after a while he refused to leave his land, afraid of that inevitable clap on his shoulder that meant he would be led back to prison in Russia, for if the truth be known, he'd flown the coop, turned tail, vamoosed, chickened out--or, if you need to be poked in the eye with it, deserted from the Russian cavalry.

During his years of service fighting for the Czar, everyone called him Friederich the Wild, partly because his comrades thought of him and his horse, a snow-white stallion named Wild, as inseparable, and partly because of his occasional reckless feats of valor on the battlefield. After the famous battle of Plevna Bridge during the Russo-Turkish War of 1878, when he made a headlong charge into the teeth of Turkish gunfire, his horse was garlanded with acacia blossoms and put out to stud; at the same time Friederich himself received, along with a gold medal for Extraordinary Valor in Defense of Mother Russia and a handshake from the Czar himself, a month's leave in his home village near the Black Sea, during which time he promptly deserted. Along with his wife

Phillibina and their only child, a son named Fortunato in anticipation of a new life in a new land, Friederich retraced the route back to Germany that his ancestors had taken when they colonized in Russia two generations before; and then on *The Crown Prince Wilhelm* out of Hamburg, they embarked for America.

That first day heading for America, Friederich began his metamorphosis. From a deck-side winch he appropriated some grease to tame his wild head of hair, for once in his home village of Rossberg he had been known as "Hen's Nest" because of his unruly mop. To mask his soldierly stride and give himself a limp, he stuck stones in his boots. And, except for his wife and child, he tossed overboard most of the remnants of his other life. While the high waves of the Atlantic beat against the sides of the ship, he got rid of his army paybook and documents; tossed his saber and his fur cap with the Russian eagle spreading its wings; jettisoned his penchant for telling stories, anecdotes and ribald jokes, along with his proverbs, apothegms and "spruchworts,"--in short his entire mass of accumulated peasant wisdom, along with his nickname "The Wild,"--all, I say all, went into the drink.

Then to remind himself never to give away his real identity, to keep quiet and "halts maul" and to mangle the soft endings and sweet sounds of his native dialect if he ever did speak up, Friederich inserted between his cheek and gum, like it was a never-ending pinch of snuff, that medal he'd received from the Czar (a fact he finally admitted seventy-five years later when in his dotage he shakily stood at a family reunion in the New Odessa City Park and unstoppered himself: first removing that medal from where it had so long resided, holding it up for one and all to see how it was covered with the patina of time and his teethmarks; and then in a squeaky voice, barely used in all those long years in America, a voice that after being oiled with several straight shots of peppermint schnapps turned into the strong melodic tones of a young man, recounted the history that his teeth had etched into that medal; telling how he'd clamped his jaw hard to make this mark when he learned Slavak had stolen a horse and been put into the state pen; how, when and where he'd lost this finger in the straw chopper or bale elevator or that finger when Slavak--who was always getting things mixed up, thought Friederich said "go" when he really had said "whoa,"--let out the clutch in the tractor while Friederich still had his finger in the hitch; or how he'd bit hard when he heard I'd received my draft notice during the Viet Nam war).

Friederich and Phillibina got off the wagon that day of the Indian scare; and, with little Slavak darting ahead of them trying to catch his father's elongated shadow in that of the chicken snitcher, they all walked along the one block main street of New Odessa with its tarpaper shacks, sodhouses, and occasional frame buildings, a tiny settlement which would later become the county seat, a place that Friederich, once he learned English, would (in one of the few lapses from his self-imposed silence) always call "the horse's ass."

There were wagons heaped with hurriedly gathered belongings just like their own, and in one wagon Friederich saw a gilt-edged picture of the Czar that made him shudder. Livestock milled about, chickens, geese and cattle, and in the mud between the buildings on the main street, there were children

14

riding on each others' backs, in opposing armies, pulling each other into the muck and acting out the drama of the Indian attack that everyone expected. Along the wooden sidewalk, gathered together into small, nervous clumps, Friederich and Phillibina could see their countrymen, "unsera leuta," as they called themselves, our people, the Black Sea Germans, in their colorful shawls and scarves and fur hats, everyone worried about what they were going to do when the Indians attacked. Probably none of them had ever seen an Indian, but all had heard stories of what had happened to Minnesota settlers a few years before; and most of the immigrants knew firsthand what had happened on the steppes of Russia when Kirghiz and Tatars had kidnapped and raped and murdered, and assumed that the American equivalents of these tribesmen would only do the same.

Slowly Friederich made his way around the settlement, staying just within earshot of the conversations. He could hear the soft rolling musical tongue of people from the Sarata colonies, and the slow, sure, rounded endings of every word uttered by the settlers from the Rohrback region, and the broad accented words of the colonists from Arcis--that stew of languages being ladled out here on the plains of Dakota Territory made him feel almost as if he were at home. But he could also sense fear and tell that no one wanted to assume responsibility for leadership; too many people had their own ideas about what should be done. Some wanted to form a well-guarded wagon train and head for safety overland to Fort Lincoln, where there were soldiers garrisoned. Others wanted to gather militia and ride out to meet the Indians head-on. Many thought it best to remain in town and defend the terrain there as best they could. In the middle of this fracas, trying to make sense of the arguments in the various tongues and dialects, and trying to keep some order among these "Rooshans" with their prognathous faces and squat bodies and rough manners, was the red-faced Yankee storekeeper Seamus McCogy.

When Friederich and his family had arrived too late that first year for planting, McCogy had graciously extended them credit; and that next Fourth of July, anxious to pay the storekeeper back, Friederich was the first to volunteer, when a traveling side show of painted wagons and strange acts came to New Odessa, to try to win a ten dollar gold purse offered to anyone who could stay for three minutes in the ring with Wrestler Gamble, a hulking, shaven-headed fellow who hissed challenges at the crowd in broken English.

Shucking his shirt that hot summer day as he climbed into the makeshift ring, Friederich tried hard to remember the footwork and choreography of the wrestling holds he'd learned as a member of the Czar's personal bodyguard. He quietly removed from his finger a gold ring of entwined serpents that his father had found plowing near some ancient Scythian burial mounds overlooking the Black Sea--a ring that in later years was used by our family as a cure for jaundice, hives and ringworm, and to keep Spanish influenza at bay during the epidemic; and once great-aunt Sophie had been forced to wear it in an ineffective attempt to quell her fibs about the family events she claimed she'd witnessed; and much later that same ring was taped to fit my own baby fingers, when my

16

grandmother was trying to rid me of my recurrent urges to wail and blubber in English. I say, that after removing his ring, Friederich promptly won the prize money, dispatching the hulking Gamble in less than a minute, despite the fact that his opponent had been liberally smeared with goose-grease.

McCogy was official timekeeper of the match. He held his pocketwatch in the palm of his hand like it was a broken egg yolk as he watched Friederich in scant seconds throw Gamble out of the ring and against the tin-sided land office. Greatly impressed, the storekeeper shouted out, "He is a wild man!" and so dubbed Great-grandpa with the nickname he had so desperately tried to shed during the Atlantic crossing. In later years Sophie-Bass would insist she had watched the match too, saying she remembered the sound of Gamble hitting the land office, the rustle of the tin that sounded like thunder, and the voices of the crowd calling out their approval; but she maintained she had a hard time seeing anything that day, for whatever reason. "Maybe the air was thicker then," she said.

In winning the prize money that day, and making a public display of himself, Friederich had gambled that the Russian government wasn't fully aware of his desertion, and hadn't yet sent agents to scour the countryside looking for him; but now, two years later, he judged the situation more dangerous, and skulked around the periphery of the conversing settlers, keeping a low profile and his eyes peeled. But he couldn't hide from McCogy, who spotted him almost immediately and began to shout that he had found their man, someone who had all the qualifications to lead, who, if he could command half as good as he could fight himself, would insure their safety. "The man to lead us has come," McCogy said.

McCogy would not take no for an answer, pushing his candidate for leader ahead of him and shouting out, "Here is the wild man, here is the wild man!" Friederich glanced warily about for any sign of someone who might know of him from the old country, who might reveal his dark past, his desertion; but on all sides he was met with only approval. It is here that his vow of silence and his gold medal worked against him (he still had the coin tucked between his cheek and gum): when he tried to raise his muffled objection, everyone thought he was agreeing, and by the time there was a show of hands, he'd been unanimously selected as commander in chief of the New Odessa garrison, and was summarily given extraordinary war powers.

Now through all this Phillibina did not interfere or speak up for her beleaguered husband, knowing that the hope of the people might lie in his military skills; but after his selection, when he just shrugged his shoulders fatalistically, she was the one who seized the moment and said, "It takes courage to bake cookies, but it also takes lard." When everyone heard the old proverb, knowing that it voiced their collective wisdom concerning the task ahead, and when they raised their shouts in a hurrah of approval, which sweet-mouth do you suppose by this time had finished licking the jelly clean from his face, and took advantage of the crowd and the excitement to explore various unprotected pockets, no matter how deep, with the help of his "chicken snitcher," in a never ending quest for something sugary?

Without a moment's hesitation, Friederich began

18

to walk around New Odessa, surveying what resources he had at his command. He hoped he was not as conspicuous as he felt; perhaps there were no Russian agents scouring the area looking for him; but he could never be sure. After all, he told himself, someone had to take charge: and he had his growing family and their safety to think about.

Meanwhile Phillibina had come upon her cousin, a woman her own age who'd taken up land on the other side of New Odessa. They'd not seen each other since immigration two years before, and quickly became reacquainted while making preparations for supper. Together they built a small smoky fire adjacent to the land office--a frame building whose tin siding announced in large black letters in English and German: Cheap Land, Inquire Within. They joked about the sign, and the cheap land they'd borrowed for the evening, speculating about the Indians and reminiscing, and then enlisted their children's help. Here our Slavak had to momentarily abandon his chicken snitcher, for both hands were required, and soon everyone was rolling out between their palms egg-sized pieces of dough delved from the pillow case. They added chopped onion and pepper, and dropped their creations into bacon drippings sizzling in a frying pan over an open fire, raising their voices together in song:

> *Where is the German homeland?*
> *Wherever you are cooked*
> *Oh Schuffnudala of our hearts*
> *That stick to weary ribs.*

After pacing the town and mulling over his options to defend the place, Friederich finally returned at supper-time, at first refusing to eat, mumbling something about work tasting better than food, and wanting to get back to his job, for the Indians were sure to be coming soon. But when Phillibina brought him a plate with a flotilla of schuffnudalas sinking in gravy, who was he to refuse, to deny or begrudge, to challenge or refuse to sink his teeth with peasant efficiency into schuffnudala? It wasn't long before Friederich was dreamily chewing, his thoughts roaming the forests of family history, as he consumed each possibility, each hope, each affirmation, each schuffnudala--searching for a solution to the defense of New Odessa.

Now anyone who has ever eaten schuffnudalas, who has ever sat at table with these delights of the palate before him, knows that besides their taste, if there is anything the Black Sea German truly loves, it is their shape: the tender dough softly rounded on both ends in the ideal platonic shape for our beleaguered immigrant, a shape that gives solace in time of oppression and hard times (such as those first years in America when everyone and his grandmother was saying how filthy these wandering Germans were with their lice and stale sea-smell from the dank steerage of the ships that had brought them to the new country), and a shape that provided the model for our ancestors to build forest enclaves against the invading Roman legions, and to defend themselves against Kirghiz tribesmen on the steppes of Russia when Germans colonized there--if ever there was a shape that could be counted on, a bulwark that smacked of home and safety, it was that of our much esteemed schuffnudala.

After supper, Friederich quickly took charge of the

situation. One of his favorite expressions, borrowed from Phillibina, was "Work come here, I'll eat you up," and with an authority that belied his muffled manner, and with his gold medal properly inserted between his cheek and gum to mangle the mellifluous endings of his native dialect (Sophie-Bass always said he sounded during those harrowing days like a pig with his snout caught in a cream can)--Friederich sent riders out in all directions to watch for attackers, and gave orders that huge bonfires be lit on the highest hills in the distance should anyone be sighted. He sent several men to Fort Lincoln to gather rifles and ammunition and alert the garrison there of the situation. He ordered men from nearby farms to get their breaking plows and to begin turning over the prairie and stacking the sod. And the rest of the people in New Odessa he set to work in the twilight, moulding bullets in the blacksmith's shop, or he drilled them in the correct manner of carrying arms. Phillibina did her part too, suddenly thrust into a position of responsibility as First Lady of the Siege, organizing the women to prepare provisions to withstand the attack. As for the Slavak, he was busy wedging his snitcher between the boards of the wooden sidewalk, pulling the tendon to close the claws around several pieces of licorice that had fallen between the cracks. (And Sophie-Bass, if we can believe her, said she wanted nothing to do with the hubbub. "It was hard a day for me, and anyway, my fingers hurt from holding on," she always said later.)

Late into the night, after everyone except the sentries had gone to sleep, and only a few smouldering campfires illuminated our scene, Friederich remained awake, counting horses and weapons, and

21

enumerating the men capable of using both. When the wide "tuechle" of dawn, that colored shawl of morning, spread its first rays over the eastern horizon, Friederich, who had donned his greatcoat against the first breath of winter that was in the air, was already walking around the entire town, trying to determine the most defensible position, settling finally on a rise of land on the southern edge of town. Picture the scene then: Friederich striding purposefully along, and following behind him our little Slavak, carrying that chicken snitcher like a divining rod. One would like to say that the boy's features radiated filial respect and admiration, but if the truth be told, what drew him forward was the precious object that Friederich fondled so lovingly in that deep pocket-- something that our habitual "suessgusch" could only imagine as sugary, as sweet, as some kind of miniature paradise, for why else would his father always reach there?

After such a supper and during the long hours of the night, a shape formed itself in Friederich's thoughts, and it was that gently ovate form that he began to draw in the dirt that morning, dragging the heel of his boot around the hill to show where the walls should be built of the structure he planned. And it was little Slavak, who'd just finished a breakfast of cold schuffnudala sprinkled with bits of licorice he'd fished with his snitcher from beneath the boardwalk, who recognized and named and shouted out to gathering townspeople as the first rays of daylight slanted over New Odessa, who cried out and gave the place its irrevocable nickname as Friederich delineated the outlines: 'It looks just like a big schuffnudala!" Slavak said. And quickly, under Friederich's direction, the people fell to the task of building the fort to protect themselves against the expected attack, Fort Schuff-nudala, as it came to be known.

They loaded the sod chunks onto wagons and hauled them to the hill, stacking them in thick layers where Friederich dictated by grunting or pointing or drawing in the dirt with a stick to explain the con-struction. Everyone was set to work and whenever there was a spare moment Friederich drilled his fledgling garrison in the use of weapons: marching the men, some carrying broom handles and other pieces of lumber in place of rifles, around the fort, like Joshua's men around Jericho, only this time it was with the walls rising.

Near mid-morning Friederich noticed a man with a distinct military bearing peering in his direction and asking people questions that obviously had to do with him. The fellow was trying to find out something, and whatever it was, Friederich didn't want to know, for he threw himself with desperation into his command: if the man was a Russian agent, he reasoned, maybe the immigrants, if they found Friederich so indispen-sable in their preparations for the attack, might not allow the man, the agent, who no doubt had cohorts scattered in the crowd, to return Friederich to Russia and imprisonment. How was he to know anything, he wondered, for all this thinking was hard on someone used to backbreaking work.

By the end of the day, a deep trench was being dug around the walls, which had risen to a height of eight feet, and Friederich, greedily eyeing the railroad track that ran through New Odessa, ordered that the finishing touch be put on his creation on the crest of the hill.

Now Friederich never did like any means of transportation except horses. He intensely disliked autos, and thought them possessed of the Devil, with their willful ways and their refusal to follow his commands. (Though later he did drive a Willis Whippet, but only after cutting holes in the floorboards so he could watch the ground move as he drove and feel the grass whipping against his boots.) But he harbored his deepest hatred for trains, since in a mile-long race over frozen steppes in Russia a steam locomotive, beating his horse Wild by the length of a cow-catcher, had caused him to lose a month's wages. So in belated revenge, and to further fortify Fort Schuffnudala against attack, Friederich set a crew of men to work removing the ties from a spur of track, and had the ties set upright in the ground at intervals around the fort, with barb wire strung between.

While Friederich was watching his men bent to this task, his thoughts were in Russia. He remembered fond times with his horse Wild, the oath of allegiance he had been required to sign, that he support the Czar and Holy Mother Russia for his entire four year military tour, and the warning that any deserters would be hunted down, no matter how far they ran; and it was then, suddenly, he felt a hand on his shoulder, and there was the man from before who'd been asking questions, saying insistently, "Weren't you and didn't you and you were the Wild, how could anyone ever forget that face, and confess now."

Friederich denied more than the three Biblical times, shook his head innumerable times more, and elongating the mangled endings of his words to mimic the raucous dialect of a Kashubian he'd once heard

in the army, maintained that he wasn't the often men-
tioned hero of the Plevna Bridge, denied he was the
wild man who led charges against Turkish hordes,
denied he was this cavalryman with a deep and
abiding love for horses.

Milke, for that was Friederich's interrogator,
wouldn't take no for an answer, and as evidence of
his assertion grabbed our shaken hero by his coat (his
prized astrakhan greatcoat that had kept him safe and
warm through so many campaigns, in later years a
coat that Sophie-Bass wore in blizzards, and a coat
that I borrowed when I got my Viet Nam draft notice
and headed for Canada), and demanded to know, that
if the holes that so liberally ventilated the coat were
not from Turkish bullets, then just what were they
from. Friederich, trying to deny and defend and make
his own point all at the same time, blamed the holes
on the sparrows in this new land, saying the birds were
able to fly at terrific speeds, and some of these
creatures had managed to strike at him, but luckily
in his voluminous coat he'd been able to dodge their
deadly flight and they'd passed through the fur
without harming his flesh; and then, doubling a fist
that looked like it could blot out the sun, Friederich
said Milke should be very careful, why those same
birds just might attack him and he might not be so
lucky.

At this point Milke abandoned Friederich and
decided on another approach. He sought out the
man's son, a thin, bony, close-cropped little fellow
whom he had seen roaming the streets with a chicken
foot in his hand. Milke found the boy staring into the
mercantile store window and promised the child
some jelly beans if he would answer some questions.

Surely, Milke reasoned, it would be easy to determine from the child if his father really were the great hero of Plevna that all Russia had once talked about. To begin with, Milke said, holding out a handful of the jelly beans towards the child, they'd start off with something easy.

"Now you know what kind of an animal that is, don't you?" Milke asked the youngster, pointing to a horse harnessed to a breaking plow in the muddy main street.

"It's a haussa--a rabbit," Slavak said, eager for his reward.

(And now while Milke is taken aback by the reply, it would only be fair to point out to the reader that one day the past summer, when Phillibina wanted to work in her garden without distraction, she had given a large squash to the boy to occupy him.

"Now this is a horse egg," she said. "And who knows, if you are careful and sit on it long enough why it just might hatch."

Right there on a knoll overlooking the garden where his mother worked, our Slavak bent to his maternal task. All his senses attuned, he sat under the wide sky, his posterior positioned directly on the squash. But it wasn't long before he tired of his duty. He stood to get a better look at his father, who stood off in the distance, waist deep in the blue sheen of an alfalfa field. Then he decided to examine his egg more closely. He stroked the hard surface; bent his ear close to hear the heartbeat; kissed and spoke quietly to his would-be offspring; turned it over to look lovingly at the other side. It was then he accidentally bumped his precious possession, and had to stand helplessly while it rolled down the hill and ex-

26

ploded against a rock, behind which a large jackrab-
bit had been resting. When the rabbit ran away with
its hindquarters flying and its ears flattened, our
Slavak pursued, shouting, "Come back, horse, I am
your mother!"

Milke, hearing the boy's reply, began to have his
doubts. Perhaps his short sojourn in this new country was doing things to his mind: he could swear the
lantern-jawed fellow with the nervous twitches was
really his old comrade from the Caucasus campaigns,
the hero who so dearly loved his own horse that he
slept with it and pampered and curried it at every opportunity. But surely such a man's own son would not
go around calling horses rabbits.

The following day, as the sod wall rose to its full
height, as men began to poke their rifles through the
slots provided in the structure for firing, as the shape
of the fort more and more resembled the aforemen-
tioned schuffnudala, Friederich watched the comple-
tion of his enterprise and for an instant forgot his
worry about being recognized. But just as he was
basking in the glow of accomplishment, he heard a
voice behind him say the dreaded words, "Komma
dolly vou," and felt the long reach of the Russian Em-
pire, Czar Nicholas himself it seemed, tighten its grip
on his shoulder. The greeting was in French, or what
Friederich knew of French, the language favored by
the officer class of the Russian military; and when he
turned around there was Milke again, this time
thrusting a group photograph of the 22nd Starobeltsi
Regiment under his nose, and pointing out with his
forefinger a lantern-jawed man, wearing the requisite
leather boots, and an astrakhan greatcoat that looked only too familiar, and with a look on his face that

seemed to say, "Dort naus liegt Amerika," or "Out there is America." The fellow in question was also holding a heavy Krinkov rifle, with large Russian letters carved into the thick stock that said, "Wild."

Our Friederich admitted defeat. His defenses had been penetrated. He sat on the ground outside the walls of the fort feeling like someone had removed his spine, and in his mind's eye could see his entire American incarnation pass away: no more kids, grandchildren he'd never see, the fruit of his entire lineage withering on the vine while he languished in a Russian prison or was shot. He looked around, expecting Milke and his cohorts to descend upon him, worse than Indians, and lead him away in shackles.

But there was only Milke, hovering over him, flailing his arms and imploring Friederich that there must be complete silence about this thing; they must mention it to no one. Milke began to beat Friederich on the back in joy, saying how he could now forgive himself for deserting too, now that he found out the great hero of Plevna Bridge, the talk of the Russian army, Friederich the Wild, had also done the same thing.

Our shaken Friederich embraced his old comrade under this new sky, and the two of them sat down to recount old times. They sat talking for hours, telling each other stories, like the time Friederich had once devised a foolproof way to determine the sex of a prisoner they'd captured, who was dressed in women's clothing and wearing long hair. Without warning Friederich had tossed a coin into the prisoner's lap, and the knees went together instead of apart, as with a woman accustomed to wearing a skirt, and so they knew they had a spy on their hands. So they reminisced about incidents like this, and sometimes Friederich laughed so hard he bent double, and that medal would do a little polka step on the tiny dance floor inside his mouth.

Now little Slavak, whose appetite for sweets was only whetted by the single jelly bean begrudged him by Milke, had shadowed his father for hours, hoping to delve with his chicken snitcher into paternal pockets; and had sidled close while his father sat talking to his old comrade-in-arms, and after maneuvering and waiting for just the right moment, was about to pull the tendon and close the claws of his snitcher on a certain tobacco pouch that didn't contain tobacco.

It was this moment that Friederich chose to show his old friend what the Queen had bestowed on him years ago--that keepsake of royal cake, much the worse for wear after several years on the prairie, but still something to remind them; and as Friederich dug in deep pockets, our slavering little Slavak had to retreat, regroup and wait for another opportunity.

Later that afternoon the Indians finally came. A cloud of dust was sighted in the distance and the signal given to seek cover behind the solid walls of Fort Schuffnudala. But it was not a marauding band, and not Sitting Bull leading warriors bent on revenge, but three stragglers on spavined, bony nags, who'd quit the reservation because of hunger. They approached peacefully, first quietly surveying the great scar on the prairie where the sod had been removed to build the fort and poking inquisitively at the swaths of soil still remaining from the breaking plows. During a brief parley with Friederich and a delegation of the settlers, the newcomers made it known that the white people had turned the earth wrong side up, and after walking around the fort and pushing at its thick walls, the visitors went on their way again, and that was the end of the Indian scare.

One by one the relieved immigrants hitched up their wagons and gathered their belongings, abandoning their fort and heading for home. Phillibina took her pillow case with what remained of her bread dough, while Friederich exchanged goodbyes and "machst guts" with Milke. When the two comrades vowed to see one another soon, a broad smile, with a gleam of gold, spread itself over Friederich's face. For the long ride home Slavak sat on the front seat of the wagon, strategically sandwiched between Friederich and Phillibina. We don't know much about this journey to the homestead, for Sophie-Bass says she slept most of the way, "except when we hit that buffalo wallow and those damn rocks."

But what shape, what position do you suppose Sophie the Endless assumed in her slumbers but that of our schuffnudala, our much esteemed schuffnudala, and what do you suppose everyone had for supper when they got home with the remnants of dough in the pillow case? And what, just what do you think our little Slavak had for dessert?

Roping the Moon

That summer before my sixth grade year strange men showed up in town. They sat in the Magpie Cafe for lunch, struggling to read the German dishes on the menu; and in the evening you could find them in the bar, drinking cold beer and talking about their long days with their transits in the coulees and fields around New Odessa. Before long everyone knew they were a crew surveying for a high voltage line to be built through the county, and near the end of the summer the head engineer of the project, a man named Hoffman, moved to town with his family.

In school that first day I saw James Hoffman, a tall boy whose delicate features seemed out of place among the peasant faces of our class. His speech was different too, without the burr of dialect that the rest of us had from our German-speaking homes. And the way he sat, so quietly and dignified, made me want to become friends with him.

For me, books were a place where I could lose myself, press farther and farther away from myself. With no friends to speak of, I spent long hours bent over musty volumes like Ridpath's *History of the World*, filling my mind with the past. All my reading made me a good student; my teachers often complimented me on my clear and precise answers. So at the end of the first week, when the teacher asked me a question in history class, I felt my chance to impress this new boy had finally arrived.

As I stood to speak, I couldn't help myself; my imagination took over. The correct answer no longer mattered. With one gesture of my hand I arrogantly swept away thousands of years: the Bering land bridge once again spanned the distance to the New World, and Roman legions marched across. Their scarlet helmet plumes waved in the wind; the hot sun shone on their polished armor. With a hoarse shout the battle-scarred commander led his men against the half-naked savages of the plains. Vastly outnumbered, the Romans fought bravely, and then, uttering oaths of allegiance with their last breaths, fell upon their swords on the sloping pastures around New Odessa.

My teacher shook her head at my imagination. My classmates gazed at me open-mouthed, wondering where I got such a wild story. As for James Hoffman — he turned his open face towards me, watching me intently.

After school James grabbed me by the shoulder and asked if he could walk with me, since we both lived on the northern edge of town, just several blocks from each other. We had a lot of interests in common, he said, including history.

"Even if it is your own version," he said, laughing; and as we walked, he asked me about my reading and books, and that next week we spent all our time together during recess. Finally one day he asked me to his home.

My mother, who often chided me for my solitary ways, readily gave her permission.

"Everybody needs a friend," she said sadly.

My stepfather was excited; he knew of Mr. Hoffman as a powerful man, in charge of hiring and firing for the entire powerline project, and was only too ready to respect anyone with money.

"You get in with those people and they'll treat you like one of their own," he said.

The next day after school, my new friend and I walked towards his home. It was the end of summer. A carpet of leaves covered the lawns around the clapboard houses that faced the street. We passed old men in dark vests and short-billed caps, who tended smoky fires with rakes, and old women in worn dresses bending stiffly from the waist to gather dried garden stalks and vines for the fires. Then we came to his house, one of the few in town built of brick; it stood far back from the street, with awnings hooding the windows.

Inside, it was nothing like my own home; I drank in everything greedily. Colorful handwoven carpets covered the polished hardwood floors. Copper bowls and figurines of Hindu gods stood on the end tables. In the bookcases and on the shelves that lined the walls, everywhere I looked, there were books: more than the town library, books about travel, art, music — a treasure trove.

James showed me his room, where he kept his boomerangs, kites, his science-fiction books, and the ancient stone tools and pottery fragments that he and his father had found at archaeological sites they'd visited in their travels.

When we went back to the living room, I was startled and nervous to see Mr. Hoffman in a wicker chair. He'd entered the house quietly, I hadn't even heard him. He was reading a thick newspaper from New York that made the *New Odessa Star*, with its several pages of uneven linotyped columns of print, seem pathetic, like a child's first book.

Mr. Hoffman shook my hand, while Mrs. Hoffman, who was quietly preparing supper along the gleaming chrome sinks and countertops of the kitchen, called out, "It's so good to have you visit."

For supper we sat at a table with carved wooden legs. Through the leaded glass windows the dying sun cast its rays, striking the heavy rings on Mr. Hoffman's fingers, the cameo that Mrs. Hoffman wore on her taffeta dress, the amber comb that swept her hair back from her placid face. The conversation moved around me as I ate: they listened to each other, they didn't interrupt, and even James spoke. They talked about the countries where they'd lived, the different projects that Hoffman had worked on, dams in faraway places like Egypt and Peru--all with a civility and decorum unknown to me.

"Now why don't you tell us about your family and these people in New Odessa," Mr. Hoffman said, turning to me. He said he knew the people in town spoke German, yet many had been born in Russia, and he wanted to know more.

I began to tell about my Grandfather Netzer and his birthplace in the dusty little German colony along the Black Sea. While I spoke, I felt a surge of pride in just knowing the Hoffmans, just sitting at their table; and wondering what I could offer them for their hospitality, for everything, I began to make up stories.

Grandpa Netzer, after coming to America as a child, had never left the county; but I claimed he had led a life of adventure, winning and losing fortunes, once owning a Bolivian silver mine, fighting wild Kirghiz tribesmen in Asia, and that as a heroic member of the Czar's personal bodyguard he had befriended the Queen of all the Russias. My imagination carried me along and I said she had once given him as a present a beautiful ivory comb, inlaid with emeralds and lapis lazuli, as if just in my telling I could redeem my poor family. I didn't stop with Grandpa Netzer; I transformed my stepfather into a hero too. His sunken chest disappeared, his shoulders widened, and with bandoliers of ammunition he charged into Nazi machine gun fire during the Battle of the Bulge.

After the meal, his parents asked me to return sometime and tell them more. Outside, James and I stood on the street in front of their house. James told me he wanted to become an archaeologist, like Schliemann who found the walls of Troy, or Carter who found the mummy of Tutankhamen. But to do that he would need a good education, he said, and after his father and the work crews finished the power line project, sometime during the next year, his family would move east. There he would attend a private school to prepare for college.

I confessed that my own plans were not so definite. My stepfather wanted me to learn how to install linoleum and carpets, like he did. "As long as people walk, they'll need you to cover their floors," he said.

Then James asked to visit me the next Saturday and meet the members of my family I had spoken so much about. I hastily agreed; but walking home, filled with happiness as I thought of my new friend and his parents, and of our evening together, I also

35

wondered what to do.

The dark night, spreading itself over the town, pressed down on me. Nothing, not much anyway, of what I had told the Hoffmans about my family was true. But the truth was probably more complicated than anything I could have made up; at my age I just couldn't get a grasp of our tangled lives.

My mother's divorce was a forbidden topic, along with any mention of my real father. Only later would I learn of his wandering life as a professional baseball player and musician, of his near starvation in a Nazi prisoner of war camp, or the duets he sang over WDAY radio with an aspiring songstress who would take the name Peggy Lee.

And sometimes an old man appeared at our door, waving his hands wildly and demanding in German to see his grandchildren. I believed what my mother always insisted; that he was just an old crazy drunk and certainly no relative of ours. Later, I would find out he was my Grandfather Rossler, a convicted horsethief, and a bootlegger who during prohibition once swam the Missouri River to escape federal agents who'd caught him peddling homemade corn whiskey in the alleys of New Odessa. I would also hear the dark rumors that after serving time in the state penitentiary, he had set fire to the old state capitol building in Bismarck, leaving it a smoking, charred ruin.

The Netzers, an aging couple I called Grandma and Grandpa, lived in the back part of our house, in two small rooms that smelled of liniment. They were my stepfather's parents, and always seemed to be arguing; their bickering shook the house. Saturdays were the worst. Grandpa Netzer would pull his battered slouch hat over his eyes and let Grandma rail about all the bitter disappointments of their married life.

Grandma Netzer's noisy religious manias, which grew worse whenever she read the Bible, ruled her life. Everywhere she looked she saw signs of the coming end of the world. Every year, in the red harvest moon, she saw the blood prophesied in Revelations. "The moon is blood. It's the end--alles fertig," she would say.

Most people in New Odessa avoided Grandpa Netzer, and some thought he was crazy. Often, he defended Adolf Hitler, and praised all the wonderful things the man had done for Germany. He had even named our rooster after the dictator, and when he dumped table scraps over the fence for our chickens, he would call out, "Adi, Adi, it is your friend Netzer." Never able to stand up to Grandma, he would bait anyone who tried to criticize Hitler for starting the war or for killing six million Jews. "Yah and I suppose you are perfect?" he would say. As for Jews, Grandpa Netzer knew only one, a Mr. Mackovsky, who showed up in town only once a year to collect his land rent; and sometimes he would wave his hat towards the open prairies and say, "Oi, where would they ever find that many Juta to kill anyhow?"

My mother was the only member of my family I wanted James to meet. On bad days, when she had to ride out my stepfather's tantrums over her spending too much money, or when everyone was arguing, she would wring her apron in her fists and stare off into space, helpless. When I told her about James' visit, she quickly agreed to help with preparations, and for the occasion to bake blachenda, a sweet Russian pastry with pumpkin filling.

"Yah maybe your friend will like my blachenda as much as you do," she said.

My mother agreed to get Grandma Netzer working in the garden for the afternoon, and to keep Grandpa Netzer busy too. It was time again, she said, to send him over to Alois Zimmerman's pedal grinding stone to sharpen the knives we used to butcher the chickens penned in our backyard. She'd make certain, she said, that he had a thermos of strong coffee so he'd stay all afternoon.

"Why those two old guys will talk the afternoon away," she said. "And if you hide Grandma's Bible so she can't get excited, it will all work out."

After lunch on Saturday everything was set for my friend's visit. My mother, pleased that she might have a quiet afternoon, was rolling out the dough for the blachendas. Grandma Netzer was in the garden, raking together dried stalks and vines, when I slid her cherished Bible between some religious magazines under her bed. And before my mother had packed off Grandpa Netzer with his knives, I'd spiked the coffee in his thermos with some of my stepfather's whiskey. I thought something stronger than coffee would keep him from wandering back to our house early to cause trouble.

Everything was going as planned. After Grandma and Grandpa left, I walked to Hoffmans', to accompany James to my house, and make certain he arrived at the right time. Walking along the road's edge, I could feel the first breath of winter in the air. The dry weeds of summer swept at our jackets. When we came to our house, a strange car was parked along the curb. James seemed to wince as I led him through the "vorhausel," a shabby entryway built onto our

38

home from some discarded lumber. Once inside I expected the wonderful smells of baking pumpkin. But on the stove top there were only greased, empty trays, and bowls of filling and dough--unbaked.

In the living room I could hear the door-to-door salesman's pitch. He was offering on low monthly payments a new sewing machine, something my mother coveted.

"Only eight dollars a month--you can save that from your grocery money," the salesman was saying.

"Maybe," my mother said.

Her loneliness made her an easy mark for peddlers. If they got inside they could sell her anything. After the Netzers moved into our house, no one visited her anymore. She seemed unable to disagree with anyone in her own living room, for fear they would think ill of her or leave her.

I was uneasy. My plans had been to keep James entertained from the time he crossed our threshhold. The blachendas were to have been the first part of my plan. I had imagined us eating our fill, relishing those pastries. I didn't want him to notice our poor home; the cigarette burns on the floors, the discolored patches that spread on the ceiling from our leaking roof.

Quickly, I began showing James my collection of arrowheads. He handled each one, holding them up to the light to admire their outlines and chipping. Seeing them in my friend's hand they no longer seemed like much: fashioned crudely from low-grade flint — I imagined the Indians who'd made them had probably been as poor as my own family.

James said he especially wanted to see that ivory comb that had once belonged to the Queen of Russia. After ducking into Grandma Netzer's bedroom and rummaging around noisily in a drawer, I returned to the kitchen.

"Grandpa Netzer is afraid to lose such a valuable thing so he hides it," I said with a shrug, showing James instead an oval photograph of Grandma Netzer's father from the bedroom wall.

"This is Grandpa Netzer," I lied, indicating the photo of the man in a Russian uniform, and when James seemed convinced, I fabricated a story of Grandpa's headlong charge on a white stallion named Wild during the coldest day of the Russian-Turkish War. As proof I dug out of the closet his old great-coat of astrakhan wool, a ragged thing that he wore during blizzards and that smelled like a wet dog. Together James and I probed the small tears in the coat that I said were bullet holes.

By this time the salesman, with a pleased look on his face, was leaving. As soon as he was out the door I introduced James to my mother. She just sat on the couch, looking at the new sewing machine set on the coffee table in front of her. When she saw James, she sighed and said in a weak voice, "It's very nice to meet my boy's new friend."

I started to panic; that far-off look in her eyes meant I was on my own. Quickly, I ran to my room and got my Ridpath's *History of the World*, which one winter day in the library I'd pushed under my parka and stolen. To get James' attention, and to try to keep him from noticing my mother's glassy look, I started to read my favorite passages, about Rome and the long-haired barbarians from the northern forests who were pillaging the Eternal City.

"Never before," I read in a loud voice, "since the days of Brennus had Rome been so terribly despoiled.

The gilded tiles were stripped from the Capitol. The Forum was robbed of its ornaments."

Pausing for effect, I glanced up from the book at James. He was staring out the living room windows: Grandpa Netzer, weaving along the sidewalk with knives in his fists and stuck under his belt, was returning home. He looked nothing like a hero, but the whiskey had rekindled his ambition. After making short work of the sharpening, he decided it was time to butcher the chickens. His voice drifted in the screen door as he talked to himself.

"Let's make blut run," he said. "Let's cut some necks."

Grandma Netzer had just killed a garter snake in the garden. We watched her come into the front yard, the limp body of the snake over the end of the hoe that she poked at Grandpa Netzer.

"That verdamta schlanga was as thick as my wrist!" she shouted.

She meant the time long ago, at the beginning of their marriage, when they'd tried homesteading in Montana. To keep the rattlesnakes out, Grandpa Netzer had laid ropes around the yard; and one day she'd found their youngest child crawling in the dust towards a coiled rattler.

"You said schlanga won't crawl over a rope, huh," she said. "There were schlanga all over, more schlanga than kids."

She went on to let him know once again what she thought of his ropes, of him, and how nothing he tried ever worked out, how he was like all the Netzers, a mad fool and a failure.

"Arschloch! You'd rope the moon if I let you," she added.

41

Grandpa Netzer drunkenly began to brandish his knives at her. From the living room we could hear and watch everything.

"And pass auf now, watch out. Heaven isn't blind to those sharp edges," Grandma Netzer said, warning him that if he held that knife with its cutting edge upwards he would cut the face of an angel.

"Ich geb nichts drum"--I don't care a damn--, Granpa Netzer said, waving that knife like a warrior. "Maybe I want to cut the faces of all the angels. Maybe I'll chop away at Gott himself."

I read louder to drown out their bickering. My voice quavered as I boomed out the passage:

"Barbaric vessels were heaped with gold and silver treasures. The trophies which the ages of victory had hung up in the temple of peace and the Capitol were snatched down and thrown into the heap of spoils."

As Grandpa and Grandma Netzer brought their argument inside, suddenly from the other side of the house we heard loud,sputtering sounds. Lurching into view in our front yard came that crazy old man, my Grandfather Rossler. He was blowing into an old brass bugle as loud as his missing teeth would allow. Behind the mouthpiece his face was a mask of pain and alcohol. James' proud features were pale. He began to glance around warily, like a trapped animal. We could all hear Grandma Netzer in the back room of the house. Nudged into one of her manias by the upturned knife, she slammed cupboard doors and drawers, looking for her Bible, her shrill voice echo-ing: "I hope those bleeding angels hang Netzer from the rafters of the sky--verflucht!"

Now Grandpa Rossler was drunkenly banging on the door. When he wasn't blowing that bugle, he was pouring out a stew of Russian, German and English curse words over my mother and her husband for not letting him see his grandchildren. My mother sat on the couch transfixed: staring at the new sewing machine like it would be tied around her neck before she was thrown into an ocean. She began to shake, imagining all kinds of horrors which might occur when my stepfather found out about the purchase.

James looked at me with sympathy; but there was fear in his face too. His lips quivered and he seemed ready to cry, not understanding what was happening around him. I was reciting from memory now, my favorite passage, and my own fate seemed fused with the words I spoke:

"The Niobe of nations, there she stands
   Childless and crownless in her voiceless woe
An empty urn within her withered hands,
   Whose holy dust was scattered long ago...."

Grandpa Rossler, pressing his tobacco-stained face to our window, was trying to get my mother's attention by waving a small box of matches. His hair blew in the wind. His dirty shirt flapped. His baggy pants hung on the crests of his bony hips.

"What's he shouting, what?" my mother asked in a daze.

Grandpa Netzer, who had slumped in an armchair, with the knives crossed on his chest like scepters, suddenly sat up, and smacking his lips as though enjoying himself, translated the old man's dialect: "He says Jewish lightning can't strike today."

"What's that mean, what?" my mother asked.

"And he says you are lucky--du hash gluck, verstehe?" Grandpa Netzer said.

"Lucky? What's he mean lucky?" she asked.

"He says he only has half a lightning bolt," Grandpa Netzer said, roaring with laughter.

"What is this, what's going on?" my mother said.

"Matches and kerosene--that's Jewish lightning, and he says he only has matches today, no kerosene, so you're lucky," Grandpa Netzer said.

"Thanks then, thanks for everything," James said suddenly, and before I could say anything he was out of the entryway and running away from our house. When he was finally out of sight, I tried to calm down. I found myself staring straight ahead, like my mother: all I could see were those bowls of filling and dough. Feeling like there wasn't enough air in the house for all of us, I ran out into our backyard.

From there I watched Grandpa Rossler heading home, kicking up tiny spouts of dust with his jogging sidesteps; sometimes he'd stop and blow a wheezing blast on that bugle, the sounds drifting over the prairie.

In the chicken shed where we stored our tools, I found our lawn shears. Wedging the handles near the middle hinge, between the door and frame, I set the sharp points against the hollow at the base of my neck. Leghorns nesting on their eggs watched me sleepily. Hitler, the strutting rooster, scratched the dirt outside the door. As I tried to lean into the blades, the door pushed open and the shears fell.

Grandma Netzer, on her way to burn that snake in the garbage can, had found me. She saw the shears on the floor and me kneeling there. "Lieba kind"--my dear child--, she said, the hoarse whisper sliding between her lips. "I have a gift for you!" I started to look up, feeling pity for everything that slid around me in a blur: for Grandma Netzer with her stockings bagged around her swollen ankles; for those chickens in their nests, so close to death; even for that limp snake she held in her work gloves.

'Ein shaynas halsband"--a beautiful necklace--, she said scornfully, leaning over to fit that snake around my neck like a noose; and I knew she'd worked the truth from my mother about my hiding the Bible. "To wear until your end really comes," she added.

I started to run. I ran past our house, where my mother, who'd thrown open the screen door on its screeching hinges, was shouting my name. Off in the distance Grandpa Rossler sounded a raucous, drunken blast on his bugle. Along the road edge dead weeds swept at me, while the pastureland beyond New Odessa tilted and dipped, and ahead stood Hoffman's house, those hooded windows watching me.

The Second Coming of

Manley Bosch

Each day at dawn Kenny Klein waited on the outskirts of New Odessa for his cousin Manley Bosch. Sometimes he stood in the middle of the highway like a statue, and sometimes he threw his head back in despair and raised his arms, wiggling his sausage-like fingers in the air, pleading to angles of geese overhead, or just to the mute sky: "When iss Manley kumming home, when when when."

But it was always the same. The sun always rose. And Kenny took one last look down the empty highway before waddling back into New Odessa, his hometown. He went past the low, clapboard houses and along the one block main street to his tiny room above the butcher shop, where he sat on his bed, his hands trapped between his thighs until it was time for work.

Kenny was delivery boy for the only grocery store in town, depositing every check in his savings account, and living off his earnings from part-time jobs, like shoveling snow or raking leaves. He was short and fat; his bald head stuck out of his white coveralls like a wiener wrapped in too much dough. He was fifty-three years old, no longer a boy, even if he did stay up late, his weak eyes watering as he was drawn into comic books about superheroes and their enemies, whom he called "willains." And Kenny often saw his cousin Manley Bosch in his dreams: he had the muscular costumed body of Blackhawk or Captain America and swooped out of the sky to rescue Kenny from danger, time and again.

Each December Kenny made extra money delivering Christmas presents, but he didn't like Christmas. He didn't like the way the children teased him, calling him Santa Klein, and he didn't like the way they asked him to laugh so they could watch his belly shake like a bowl of jello. Often he wondered how Manley managed night after night, with big audiences watching his every move, listening to every note he played. It must be like Christmas all year around for Manley, Kenny decided.

When Kenny's cousin Manley was born, Manley's father, whose name was Ludwig Bosch, ordered a special accordion inlaid with rhinestones spelling out Manley's full name: MANLEY CLARENCE VOLK BOSCH. From the time when little Manley took his first steps, Ludwig, a hardworking farmer obsessed with the famous musician Clarence Volk, hovered over him, flailing his arms like a berserk windmill. "Practice, practice, practice," he said. "Be like Clarence Volk."

Each evening Ludwig took the young Manley to a large billboard on the edge of New Odessa, where red letters proclaimed: NEW ODESSA, NORTH DAKOTA. POP. 478. HOME OF THE FAMOUS CLARENCE VOLK. On the right side of the billboard there was a drawing of Volk wearing a cowboy hat and a Hawaiian shirt sequined with silver half-notes; over

48

his head a large clef floated like a halo. Then Ludwig would always hold out his hands to little Manley as if they had nails in them; dirt and axle grease were pushed deep into the pores. "Don't waste your life on the farm like me," Ludwig begged, pointing to the billboard. "Be like Clarence Volk."

Clarence Volk had left New Odessa years before and became a famous musician and conductor. He had his own television show. Every Saturday night his familiar face reassembled itself in living rooms all over the country. "Nize uff you to kum," Volk would say, sounding like he was still playing a barn dance near New Odessa. When he waved his baton, his band members raised their instruments and played the Volk theme song, "The North Dakota Polka." As he conducted, he turned to the television camera, and with his teeth gleaming as if he were wearing black-face, he said, "Yah, mighty nize uff you to kum and see Clarence."

As a boy Manley Bosch appeared at church affairs, talent shows and name-day celebrations all over the county. His hair was parted in the middle; he wore white patent leather shoes that tapped the rhythm; his short, square fingers struggled to reach the keys. The rest of him, hidden behind the accordion, looked like it was clamped in the jaws of a hungry shark, while he played polkas and schottisches, pulling people onto the dance floor and spinning them around like a precocious Clarence Volk.

In school, students waddled around him like they had accordions strapped to their chests, and wiggling their fingers in the air, shouted at him, "Play us a tune Manley, a hot one!" Manley quit school after the seventh grade, forming his own band, which he called "The Bubbling Four." He was the only member, and wore leather belts, jammed with harmonicas, that crossed his chest like the bandoliers of a Mexican revolutionary.

The year that Kenny and Manley both turned fifteen, Kenny began to ride along with Manley to all the dances, carrying the accordion into each dance hall and running his hands over the wooden benches and chairs to check for snags that could tear stockings and dresses. Before each performance he shuffled onstage with a fedora just like Manley's. His voice hissed through the space of his missing tooth as he said, "Here we haf my kussin to play a few toonz." Manley was hidden in the shadows at the back of the stage, his talcumed fingers poised in readiness. "All right, steam up the windows, Manley," Kenny said, and then Manley would step forward into the light, his fingers flashing over the keys.

After a dance on Manley's seventeenth birthday, Kenny hugged him and said, "You played real gut tonight. You really steamed them windows." Manley plucked his suspenders in embarrassment. Later, parked along a desolate section line miles from town, they celebrated by sharing a pint of cherry sloe gin. Manley talked about when he would be famous like Clarence Volk and how he would return to take care of Kenny. "No sirree, no poorhouse for my cousin," Manley said. After several sips of the liquor, Kenny, his lips red, laid his forehead against the cool of the car window, the lights of distant farms spinning around him while Manley finished the bottle. Very late that night, Kenny awoke suddenly: Manley was speeding back to town, the equipment trailer swaying wildly behind them. And Manley was staring at the road like he was watching a forbidden movie, one in which Kenny had no part.

On the last day of May in the New Odessa high school gymnasium, Kenny was sprinkling corn meal over the floor so it would be smooth for the prom dance that night. The dance hadn't started when a stranger in a dark herringbone suit strode by him and took a chair near the stage. Frightened, Kenny ran up to Manley, who was getting ready to play, pointed to the man and whispered, "I tink we haf trouble." Manley nodded slowly, like there was a secret inside his head that he didn't want to jar loose. That night Manley played fiercely, better than Kenny had ever heard him, with every run and flourish and all stops out, and the high school couples whirled happily under the colored bunting. But Kenny hardly enjoyed the music; he sat two chairs down from the stranger, watching him carefully, sweat pearling his upper lip. At the first intermission, Kenny bounded onto the stage with clenched fists, as if to protect Manley. The stranger followed, saying to Manley, "You play mighty nize." Finally Kenny realized who it was: Volk, *the* Clarence Volk, vacationing in New Odessa. "Choin the House of Volk," Volk said, handing Manley a train ticket. After Volk left, Kenny said he had known all along it was him. Though he had been so foolish, Kenny was happy. Manley, his friend and cousin, had taken the first giant step and become a member of the Volk orchestra.

Later that summer, Kenny was at the depot to see Manley off. He threw his arms around Manley, squeezing him as if he were a set of bagpipes. "Don't forget us little fishes back here in the pont," he whispered, tears rolling over the hummocks of his cheeks.

51

Manley only nodded, pushing the battered accordion case, his only luggage, ahead of him as he boarded the Aberdeen train to join Volk on an extended cross-country tour.

Each evening of the next month, Kenny could be found knocking on the doors of the city council members, saying, "I bring you gut tidings uff great choy," and then explaining to each member why he thought the city should hire a sign painter to make additions to the billboard outside town. Tired of answering their doors each evening and finding Kenny, the council finally relented, and voted in his favor by a narrow margin. Kenny was there at the meeting, and when the final vote was cast, he shouted out in triumph, "Don't get into a peeing match with a skonk like me."

The next week Kenny watched the sign painter add the words AND HOME OF THE FABULOUS MANLEY BOSCH to the billboard, along with a drawing of Manley wearing a bulging shirt that looked like a breastplate, and a fedora that tilted rakishly on his head. Kenny even dragged his own ladder to the billboard, climbing up to make sure everything was spelled correctly, that the word FABULOUS was twice as large as the other words, and that the drawing really was that of Manley and no one else.

From all over the country, from ballrooms with strange names, and dance halls and pavilions, Kenny received postcards from Manley. The message was always the same; When I am as great as Clarence Volk, he wrote, I will come back for you. Overjoyed, Kenny read the words over and over again, pressing his head between his hands like a vise, trying to imagine Manley and his fast-paced life.

Ludwig saw Manley perform for the first time in Volk's band on television, and it wasn't long after that the old farmer died. For the funeral, Manley returned home, driving an antique 1948 Kaiser-Frazer Deluxe with huge sun visors drooping over the windshield like the eyelids of a giant. The afternoon of the funeral Kenny looked up over the grocery box he was carrying across main street. In front of him, framed in the bright chrome of a car window, was Manley's face. It was large and fleshy, like a bloated moon. "Manley will come again for you," Manley said. Kenny, who was embarrassed that such an important person was his friend, looked away shyly. He was going to explain that his boss hadn't given him the afternoon off to attend the funeral, how he missed Manley so much, how all the words he wanted to say were tangled around his mind like string. But when he looked up again, Manley was gone and he was standing alone in the street, clutching the grocery box, his hands quivering with excitement and loss. That night Kenny dreamed, but his dreams were far away, always beyond his reach, like a visitor from another world, like that shiny blue car speeding away from him.

Manley didn't last long with Volk. He took to drinking heavily, and one night stumbled off the stage of the Trianon Ballroom in Chicago, sprawling across a table of distinguished guests, including the mayor and a senator. The next day Volk handed Manley a one-way ticket back to North Dakota. "Nize uff you to come and see Clarence," Volk said.

It didn't take long before Manley started his own group, Manley's Tyrolean Concertina Boys. But when his musicians heard the name they deserted before the first engagement. Later, Manley smeared burnt cork over his face and played with a southern band called "The Hootsy Tootsy Creoles"; he pomaded his hair and wore a red velvet matador suit, playing with Senor Juan Alvarez and his El Grande Orchestra. After that he toured with every little show band that would have him, crossing and crisscrossing the midwest, bouncing from border to border and one country bar to another.

Years passed and Kenny heard nothing from Manley. Each day he got up early, and while the sun rose, waited for his cousin outside town. All week he worked hard in the grocery store, and each Saturday night sat in the Magpie Cafe in his baggy hopsack suit. Sometimes the waitress didn't notice him and he sat until closing time, too shy to ask for coffee, and staring at the faded auction posters behind the counter. Once he sat by two farmers who bent over a newspaper photograph of Volk and his orchestra. "No Bosch in there," one farmer said, examining the face of each member. Kenny got excited. "I bet you ten to one hees got hiss own bant," he said loudly. People in the cafe pivoted on their stools and raised their heads above the booths to look at Kenny. A large drop of cold sweat dropped like a bomb from his armpit to his side and he jerked off his stool, his heavy legs churning him out of the cafe.

One day, not long after that, when Kenny came to work he found large black letters sewn across the back of his coveralls: KENNY KLEIN DELIVERY BOY. All day he thought about those words; finally, he asked his boss, Jake Manke, to change the boy to man. "Pretty soon you think you own the whole store," Manke told Kenny. Kenny replied that he was fifty-three years old and if that wasn't old enough to be a man, "Why then I quit this goldanged chop." Back in his own room, he collapsed on his bed, wondering how his world could have fallen apart so quickly.

At night out of the corners of his eyes he saw rats scurrying across the floor with pieces of Manley clamped in their long snouts. Sometimes he jumped out of bed and shuffled the postcards Manley had sent, as if they could foretell his future. Maybe Manley would now return to take care of him like he had promised so long ago, he thought. And sometimes he would find himself pleading out loud, "Yah tell me when Manley iss coming," while he repeated the names of each city and dance hall on the postcards like they were incantations, or magical fingers reaching into the world to find Manley. One night a blur took hold of him. The next thing he knew he was staring out over the prairie on the edge of town. It was as though he was standing on a strange island, alone, watching a huge ocean of sadness roll around him. Then he shone the yellow cone of his flashlight over the billboard, where the drawing of Volk was as bright as the day it had been painted. But the paint had peeled back from Manley's crisp fedora and now a shabby hat balanced on his cousin's head. Roosting pigeons had spattered the face with dripping colors, and someone had shot fist-size holes into the whites of the eyes: Manley now stared straight down at Kenny like a poor Jesus on a highway repent sign.

The next day, with his life savings, Kenny made a down payment on a tin-ceilinged building squeezed between the bank and the grocery store. He built booths, a long hardwood counter, and with a bandsaw cut out large plywood letters to spell KENNY'S BAR, and hung them above the door. For weeks while

55

he worked on his place, he slept in his clothes, his face flat on a table. Once he woke suddenly, lifted his head and saw himself in a mirror across the bar counter: his eyes were dark smudges; his cheeks were hollowed and gaunt; and he was gripping a beer glass as if it was the last hold before he fell into a deep pit. After that he was very nervous, pulling fistfuls of hair from his head until it looked like a poorly overgrown section of summer fallow. When he finally opened the bar he got only an occasional customer, like Winky Krenz who stopped in while checking water meters for what he called his "quiggie," and sometimes a retired farmer or two who brooded all afternoon over a single glass of beer. The only other bar in town, the Roughhouse Lounge, had live music two nights a week, the Meidinger Band, a local group who sang country music with a Germanic twang, and Kenny knew his watering hole with its bare walls and empty seats couldn't compete with them.

On the first day of summer Kenny got a postcard. His eyes bounced like ping-pong balls from one margin of the careening words to the other: Coming to do you a BIG favor. Heard about your new bar. I'll play for you July 9. For 96 percent of the gate of course. Your cousin Manley. P.S. I always said I'd come back and help you out.

From then on Kenny gave out free drinks to anyone who would come into his bar. Sometimes he stood out on the sidewalk and coaxed people to enter, or he'd wait in the alley for drinkers leaving the Roughhouse Lounge and would tell them he wanted them to compare his drinks, free of course, with those in the Roughhouse. When he got a new customer seated, all he could talk about was Manley's return for the grand opening of Kenny's Bar. "Who knows," Kenny said over and over, "maybe Clarence Volk kumms wit Manley too." The rumours circulated quickly, and the day Manley was to arrive, Kenny's Bar was crowded with people, all anxiously awaiting Clarence Volk.

In the middle of the afternoon an old rust-spotted Plymouth with a broken aerial limped to a stop behind Kenny's Bar. A fat man squeezed himself through the back door, and Kenny Klein immediately hugged the man, swinging him around like an oversized grocery box before leading him proudly around the bar. "Here he iss -- my cussin," Kenny announced. But no one looked at the sweaty man, for they were too busy stretching their necks over the beer signs in the front windows to see if the great Volk was coming down the main street.

For the rest of the afternoon, while Winky Krenz tended bar for Kenny, the cousins sat at a table near the back, reminiscing. Whenever Kenny asked about Volk and life "in the bik time," Manley just drained his drink, tipping his head back like a pump handle and then pushing his empty glass under Kenny's nose, saying, "How about another. You buying ain't you." Then he wrapped his legs around the base of the barstool and drank steadily, while Kenny, to reinforce the low, makeshift stage he'd built near the dance floor, pounded some extra nails, hoping it would hold his cousin's weight. At eight o'clock Manley wobbled back to the dance floor, and when it was time to play, Kenny tried his best to remember the way things used to be. "Steam up them windows Manley!" Kenny yelled across the bar as Manley slipped on his accordion, and it seemed just like old times.

57

Manley played all the old Volk favorites and the crowd responded. They hung their heads when he played "There's a Blue Circle 'Round My Heart." They pounded their knees against the bar and invaded the dance floor when he played "The North Dakota Polka." Widows with helmet-like hairdos pulled nervous bachelors onto the floor; bandy-legged farmers sashayed with their squat wives in taffeta Sunday dresses. In front of the bar, children bounced off the sidewalk like popcorn, trying to see over the beer signs and watch the commotion inside. In the dimly lit bar the brim of Manley's fedora grew long, and he could have been the great Volk the way the gay melodies rose around him, the way he swayed from side to side.

During the first intermission Manley threw ice cubes from his empty drink across the bar, and one smacked Kenny in the back of his head. Kenny knew Manley wanted another drink, a double or a triple this time, and not wanting this evening of entertainment and his grand opening to be a failure with a drunken musician, Kenny at first ignored the summons. "Yah I tink I haf to get my roof fixed maybe," he joked when the next ice cube smacked him. When he turned around the next time, still busily filling drinks, Manley was growling from behind the customers lined at the bar: "Hey fatman, bring the great Bosch another drink, pronto!" The crowd hushed, while Kenny looked up and shook his head. "No, I tink you hat enough to sink the Bismarck tonight."

By then Manley had shed his accordion and was elbowing his way to the bar, head bobbing like a snake ready to strike. "All Manley did for you," Manley hollered, clawing the T-shirt from Kenny's back.

58

Staggering backwards Manley waved a piece of the T-shirt like a truce flag. He was staring beyond Kenny at Volk's smiling face rolling over the screen of the television on the counter. It was nine o'clock and someone had turned on the set to watch the Clarence Volk Show. "Mighty nize uff you to kumm and see Clarence," Volk was saying.

Kenny worked his way through the crowd and outside into the alley, but by then Manley was gone. He could see a pair of taillights swaying wildly into the darkness east of town. In the dirt lay Manley's fedora, like Manley had been swooped away by Captain America. Behind him Kenny could hear polka music blaring and the shuffle of people dancing to the television music of Clarence Volk.

Kenny walked along the highway and went out into a hayfield, from where he dragged bales to the base of the billboard with Manley's portrait on it. On his hands and knees, his fingers cupped around a match, he let a tiny flame grow. It slowly licked over the bales, higher and higher, until ragged shreds of fire swept over the billboard and the lettering and the faces of Volk and Bosch, charring them beyond recognition. As Kenny walked heavily back into town, the billboard collapsed behind him, and a shower of sparks rose, floating over him like a hand. Kenny kept walking back to his bar, and as he walked he thought he heard music, not Manley's anymore, but his own.

Her Week of the Jew

Once a year the Jew came to town. It was in the fall that we always saw him: after the farm trucks brought their loads of grain to the town's only elevator. The train left him on the depot platform, where he would stand, holding his cloth-covered suitcase, and blinking his watery eyes. Then, he would make his way along the gravel road he called "my Via Dolorosa" to The Plainsman Hotel, a small, stuccoed building at the north end of the main street, not far from Eva's home.

The man's name was Mr. Mackovsky. He was old. A gold tooth gleamed in his upper jaw: evidence of the Jew's greed, or so Eva's husband told her. People saw that tooth a lot, since Mackovsky, who was somewhat exuberant by nature, often threw his head back in raucous laughter.

With her children finally away at college, the loneliness of her home had overtaken Eva, and so she began a job as chambermaid at The Plainsman Hotel. Soon, her face had color again. Her complaints about her ailments and pains had ceased. And she began to meet people whose paths would never otherwise have crossed hers. Sometimes campaigning politi-

61

cians took an overnight room. And there were railroad men from across the state, with their leather satchels and strange hours. But of all the people who stayed at the hotel, her favorite was Mr. Mackovsky. During her week of the Jew, for that was what her husband called Mackovsky's annual visit, she was particularly happy. Often, while doing dishes or ironing, she sang aloud her favorite song, "All Over the World," by Nat King Cole, and her husband would turn away in disgust and say, "Don't you ever get tired of that darkie's song?" Afterwards, feeling guilty about her cheerful self-indulgence, she sang her version of "Gott isch die Liebe," the somber German tune that required a pious church falsetto.

Every year Mackovsky returned. There in the autumn he would stand, holding in his hand the cloth suitcase, threadbare with the years, and, as he walked to the hotel, calling out his optimistic greetings. Sometimes he cajoled people to speak with him, saying, "I hang my heart on a hook and no one bites," or, if he stumbled on the rough gravel road, shouting at a passing car, "A snake and a Jew could break their backs crawling the ruts of this low-rent Eden." Eva never got much chance to speak with him at length. But in their chance encounters, in the hallway of The Plainsman, or on main street, he heaped her with praise. Once in the grocery store, while she stood at the checkout line, he pushed through the door and told everyone how Eva's soul was the peg that held the edge of town to the prairie and how without her the twelve hundred souls of New Odessa would spill into the wild cattle country to the north, "like a skewered water skin," he said.

Though he sometimes embarrassed her, she enjoyed the attention. Often she wished he was a permanent hotel guest, there every morning to compliment her lithe figure and quick mind, and tell her again how her voice suited a Maria Callas, the great opera singer. Through the years he began to represent for her everything that was fine and noble. And when she looked at her husband she sometimes could see only the dark aura of all their years together.

Usually there was a balance between her and her husband, a precarious one: she sensed how much she could say, confide. Unimaginative, he often saw only the words she put before him, like a prepared meal. He said little, preferring to listen to her, to sit in silence, or to just speak in a dialect, in proverbs and "spruchworts," especially when he felt she had spoken too long. "You're trying to catch the rain in a sieve," he would say, or, "An empty barrel makes the most noise."

Once, when her oldest daughter telephoned to confide in her about a new boyfriend, Eva was swept away with happiness, and told everything she knew about Mackovsky: how the man returned to The Plainsman every day after his lunch in the Magpie Cafe, and showed his appreciation for his clean room by calling her his veritable handmaiden of the azure heavens, or his own savory delight of this spinning earth. She told how when he saw her sweeping or vacuuming he said she was his "seraphim of the dustpans," and she related with an exuberance that seemed to her borrowed from Mackovsky, how in the afternoon after his nap, a big-finned Plymouth belonging to his main renter glided to the curb of the hotel and whisked Mackovsky away like a dignitary, as he visited one of his many farms.

It was the week after Mackovsky had made his visit. He was gone again, and she threw herself into her work at The Plainsman, remembering how he had bowed so regally to her in the hallway, and his words came back to her with such force that she again basked in his compliments, "My Queen Mother of New Odessa," he'd called her, and "My incandescent Czarina burning wild in the forests of my dotage." That week a bearded geologist from the state university came to stay at The Plainsman. She was feeling particularly lonely, and surprising even herself with her boldness, she asked him about his business. He told her that several miles outside New Odessa he was studying some terminal moraines, glacial deposits from the last ice age. And one rainy day while she emptied the ashtrays and vacuumed the armchairs in the lobby, the professor told her about the ancient glacier that had once covered the town and the entire countryside. Over a long time, he said, the climate gradually warmed, the glacier retreated, and the flood waters from melting ice changed the face of the land, carving deep drainage channels and depositing rolling hills.

What the professor said gripped her imagination; why, she couldn't understand. But at supper that evening she tried to tell her husband about the glacier. As she told of the geologist describing the ice age and the glacier, as she talked excitedly about the incredible changes the melting flood waters had made on the land around New Odessa, he became very angry.

After supper he left the house. Through the window she watched him walk along the sidewalk, his jaw still rigid, his angry silence turning over and over in her thoughts. She looked across the street, this last one on the edge of town, to the rusting farm equipment, the gleaners and rakes and combines abandoned in the open, weeded lot there, and saw past the grain elevator at the far edge, to the rolling pastures beyond New Odessa; and felt she knew what it was like under the weight and tremendous pressure of that ancient glacier that had once covered the land.

Though Eva was on the nervous side — she knew that, everyone told her so — after that incident she was worse. That next Sunday after church on the parsonage lawn, she watched a toddler put a fistful of dirt in its mouth. Stella Grobel, the choir director, was standing beside her. Eva turned and started telling her about a similar incident from her own childhood: how she could still almost feel the pebbles at the root of her tongue. "You would remember something ugly like that," Stella had said. "You're different you know." Eva's reply had come almost without her being aware of it, had erupted from her, and was a direct attack on Stella's refusal to pay the stipend the church council had recommended to Eva for playing the organ each Sunday. "And it looks like I'm still eating dirt too," Eva had said.

Of course she knew what townspeople said about Mackovsky: that he had quite a "gusch" or mouth, that it must be smeared with goosegrease, as the old saying goes, since he talked so much. And she also knew that many people didn't like his manner, or the disruption his visit caused. Edna Manke, the dishevelled cook at the Magpie Cafe, whom Mackovsky called his holy omnipotent angel of the cookstove because he liked her homecooked meals and especially her sugar cookies, would sniff and reply, "An ugly old thing like me, with this big nose, an angel, forget it." And just

65

the past year Mackovsky had created a stir. One Saturday night he'd stopped a child heading to get a bag of popcorn from Hiller's popcorn stand, a madeover icehouse squeezed between the hardware store and the bar on the main street. With a crowd of shoppers and onlookers watching nervously, Mackovsky asked the barefoot child if he wasn't glad there was a sidewalk beneath his feet; and asked him if he knew that it had been built by Franklin Roosevelt's WPA, despite the fact that everyone in New Odessa thought the president was a communist; and told the boy that if it wasn't for the sidewalk, why at that very moment, everyone there would be ankle-deep in mud, "and Chinamen would be licking the soles of our feet," he said.

Mackovsky had grown louder through the years. At the slightest reply to his greetings of "Hail Citizen," or "Speak Pilgrim," he grabbed people by their sleeves, and made wild motions in the air with his hands as he spoke, like he was trying to talk color and movement into all he could not see. It was thought he had some eye-disease, some ventured glaucoma; but even Christina, the widow who owned The Plainsman Hotel, and the only person allowed to administer the eyedrops he needed once a day — even she didn't know for sure what his trouble was. Eva's husband just thought that was how Jews were. Loud. Needing attention. Trying to stare into your soul.

Even with her job, Eva still had time on her hands, so she did more church and community work. Sometimes she helped neighbors. Once she offered to help Mrs. Fetzer down the block with her chicken butchering. The old woman looked at her suspiciously and asked why she was helping, and Eva had answered in dialect, almost as Mackovsky might have, she realized later, "Well someone has to oil the spokes of the world." And one evening, when she had served lunch for the Women's Society of World Service meeting in the church basement and so wasn't required to help with the dishes, she lent a hand anyway. It was then several women began to argue about the correct way to wash dishes, left to right as Edna Manke maintained, since it was the way they were done in the Magpie Cafe, or right to left as Stella Grobel insisted. Eva had stayed out of the argument, and, instead of calling her husband, decided to walk home afterwards. She walked through the early June fragrances of flowering crab bushes and lilacs. And halfway home, an emptiness opened in her that seemed as high as the dome of the sky overhead. She couldn't explain the feeling to herself, and as she crossed the highway that cut through town, with the last daylight seeping away and the air a peculiar shade of blue, it seemed to her as though the glacier had returned, that mountain of blue ice. And when she got to her house, she could not even look at her husband. She was waiting, she knew, for Mackovsky to come again.

Several months later, the Jew made his annual visit. But he mistimed his trip. Or perhaps there was a late harvest, for the evening he arrived, Eva saw trucks — a long line of them, with their tarpaulins stretched over bulging grain boxes, and backed bumper to bumper from the elevator ramp. This time, Mackovsky didn't walk. For the first time in anyone's memory, the renter's big-finned Plymouth was parked at the depot, waiting. The renter helped Mackovsky limp to the car; the renter's son, a hulking adolescent, hastily tossed the suitcase into the trunk, while Mackovsky, as always, rasped out his praises, saying, "This young man is a veritable prairie Adonis, and gracious too."

The next day at supper, the first day of Mackovsky's visit, her husband, who usually sat silently during the meal, immediately started telling about Mackovsky. Right there in front of the hardware store where he worked, he'd seen the man waylay Mrs. Springer, an elderly lady on her way to the grocery store. Mackovsky had fingered the embroidery of the woman's shawl, a "tuechla" from Russia, his fingers trailing inches from her sagging bosom, and asked if she too remembered the beauteous Russian sky, "Es war so shay," he said, or their German colonies on the edge of the Black Sea, the bursting white blossoms of the acacias, or those fine Bessarabian wines. Oh surely she remembered that land across the ocean where their childhood was lost, and surely, Mackovsky said, kissing the palm of Mrs. Springer's hand until she flushed, surely she must awaken each morning as surprised as he, "a fragile husk ready to be blown off the face of the earth by the first strong wind of mortality."

"And half the town was watching your Jew," her husband said, an accusation in his tone, for he had heard people talk about the way Mackovsky spoke to his wife.

"And what does that mean," Eva said.

"It means he wants too much. It's the way of those people," he said finally.

The week passed. Mackovsky kept to his room in the hotel. He turned visitors away from his unopened

68

door, ignored trays of food that Christina brought from the Magpie Cafe, and even refused a dozen sugar cookies that Edna Manke had baked for him. There were rumors going around town. Some said he was "verruckt," and spun their fingers at their temples. Others talked about the incident with Mrs. Springer, or how Mackovsky had managed to slip out a side door of the hotel one evening and been seen tossing fistfuls of money into the air and shouting "Let the wind eat it." And, of course, some said the old man was dead. And Eva wondered about that too, for every time she walked by his room during the week, only a pall of silence greeted her. One evening, after her husband had fallen asleep in his chair, she decided to visit Mackovsky. But on the way to the hotel, as she passed the open lot, she saw the shining eyes of an animal sliding through the long grass and weeds. Startled, she turned back and went inside thinking, "There are no secrets in New Odessa."

The next day Eva checked out some railroad men, and watched them walk along the gravel road to the depot with their leather satchels and their long-billed caps. Then she started cleaning their rooms, scrubbing their bathtubs and changing their sheets, feeling like she wanted to go see Mackovsky.

As she went about her work, she began to hear sounds, at first low and indistinct, coming from the direction of his room. Listening carefully and approaching his door, she heard Mackovsky speaking in the dialect of the Jews, the words not that different from the German she'd grown up with and still spoke. He was saying that the people of New Odessa were one of the lost tribes of Israel, fashioning from the dust of the American plains the Promised Land. And how all his people in town, "meine leuta," were saints and frozen martyrs roaming the catacombs of North Dakota in chains of ice, holy mercenaries of some new millenial ice age. And he was claiming that he was their seer and prophet, their crippled messiah, trying to deliver them from despair and the dark nights of their souls. But now, he said, his world was shrivelling like a piece of fruit, his ancient heart was laboring and tumbling in the caged sorrow of his chest, and he, Joachim Mackovsky, born in the Bessarabian village of Mayoyaroslavetz, was weary with the travails of life, and now realized he had failed, and was but skin wrapped about wind, an orphan from the green flesh of God, longing for the thick sleep of the dead.

She'd never heard such outpouring, such a rush of grief, not even during the evangelical revival week, when everyone in her church confessed their sins out loud. And listening to Mackovsky now it seemed he was giving voice to her own faded dreams.

Finally she couldn't bear it anymore, listening without his consent, and she retreated to the end of the hallway, to fold pillow cases and towels in the linen closet, but his voice seemed to follow her. In desperation she returned to the room she'd been cleaning and began to scrub down the bathroom walls until the backs of her arms ached and her nostrils burned from the cleaner. It was then she heard Mackovsky calling from his room for help with his eyedrops. "Help an old Jew mired in darkness," he said, and: "Water this withered old plant."

At first she hesitated, afraid of being alone with him in his room, and remembering what Christina had said, leaving for a funeral that afternoon, "Tell him to wait for his eyedrops until I get back." For an instant she thought it better to return to the front desk and pretend she hadn't heard; but she found herself at his door, and she heard him call out, "Enter the outpost of the lost."

She found him in his armchair by the bed, his head thrown back, his mouth open, his breath coming in sighs. There was so much she wanted to say to him: how his words and phrases had always given her strength to live another week, another year in New Odessa. But just as she was about to speak, Mackovsky motioned with a finger towards the dresser where among the bottles of liniment and salves, Eva found the small vial with the dropper. Mackovsky was staring blindly at the ceiling as she steadied her hand on his forehead, and fearful she might crush the fragile globe of his skull with her weight, she quickly squeezed a single drop into each eye.

Then he took her hand to his chest and covering it with his own, he said, "My warm gold of this world." With his chest rising and falling as though some great weight was pressing on it, he started whispering how as a child, accompanying his parents in steerage on the ship Kaiser Wilhelm der Grosse out of Hamburg in 1884 he'd eaten moldy bread, scratched lice until the blood ran in gouts from his body, watched the high waves of the Atlantic beat against the ship, and seen — "Es kummt mir nicht aus dem sinn," he said, "I can never forget it" — the immigrants' dead children, Jews and Germans alike, buried at sea. And he had seen too, he said, the grief-stricken parents scooping a handful of Russian earth from a box carried on the ship for that purpose, and depositing this in the shroud, so their offspring would not be

71

separated forever from the place of their birth, their homeland. And he told her about the visions and dreams he had of those children, lost beneath the turbulent waves, mating with whales and creating their own race there in the ocean, without their parents' love. Then, as he lapsed into sleep, he released her hand and gripped the arms of the chair as though he too were now sliding into the same watery grave.

Eva left him that way, returning to the lobby where she sat in one of the armchairs, waiting for Christina to return. Mackovsky would need his rest; in an hour or so he would be boarding the evening train. And she felt like she needed her rest too. There was a heaviness in her limbs as she stared out the lobby window: the shadows were lengthening across the lawn, the light of day was draining away. Later, when Christina returned, Eva left the hotel, crossing the main street on her way home, remembering how Mackovsky always shouted out, "Back to my Via Dolorosa," whenever he was leaving town. She found herself taking the same path, this unpaved road where the gravel was pulverized into dust from the heavy grain trucks, this same path that led to the depot and the railroad tracks.

Jack Natterud, the hard drinking depot agent, was busy behind a barricade of boxes, sorting freight and tossing boxes around in his usual cranky manner. When he didn't look up or even notice her in the waiting area, she was relieved; at least she wouldn't have to explain her presence there. She couldn't explain it to herself except that it was Mackovsky's last day, last week, last year in New Odessa — but she didn't know if she could put it into words for anyone else. Waiting, she watched the rays of the drooping sun move over the polished bench she sat on, over the whorls of oak grain that seemed themselves like suns buried in the wood.

Then the renter's son brought the suitcase into the depot; and groping his way through the entrance and fending off the closing door, Mackovsy followed, saying to the young man as he left, "Bless your ripening eyeballs my Dakota Argus, bless you." As the bench beneath her shifted and trembled, and as Eva watched Mackovsky exchange a few last words with Natterud, she knew his train had arrived.

With his suitcase in hand, Mackovsky turned to leave. It was then he seemed to see her, and throwing his head back in laughter, and his hands into the air, he called her his apocalyptic spouse of the American steppes, his Moghul princess, his high plains siren who'd shipwrecked his soul, and a host of other phrases that fell from his dry lips like rain. So this is the end of it, she thought, as he put his arms around her and slid his lips across her cheek; she felt the same as when she'd put in the eyedrops, now almost afraid that if she held him tightly his ribs might buckle or he'd crumble into dust in front of her.

After she'd watched his frail figure board the train, his suitcase pushed in front of himself as though finding his way, Eva walked home through the autumn dusk. Her long shadow moved over the rutted gravel road ahead of her, and she could hear behind her the protesting metal of the railroad tracks beneath the heavy train, and the grain cars coupling and uncoupling, their clanking sounds losing themselves in the broad meadows and carved hills beyond New Odessa. Leaving the gravel path, his path, she thought, and turning onto the street that led her home, Eva started walking more quickly, as if being carried back on waters that had once been blue ice.

Horse, I Am Your Mother

That Same Sun

That spring, when my grandfather came to live with us, he just sat in his room with the shades down, staring into the dark. So when summer began, my mother put a chair in our backyard and told him in German, "The sun will be good for you."

Each afternoon I slid Grandpa's stepped-down slippers onto his swollen feet, and with my arm under his shoulder, helped him outside. Each afternoon he just sat there, his cane across his lap, looking out at the hilly pastures north of town.

My mother explained it was my duty to keep him company. It was the least, she said, the younger generation could do.

"You'll be old someday too," she said.

"But he never says anything," I complained.

"You're only thirteen," she said. "You'll understand later."

Our new neighbor was Mr. Walth. After his wife had died, he'd retired. He'd had his small farm home jacked from its foundation and moved to town, where it was set on a new basement next to our home. Most of the past winter he had been talking about a granddaughter he had never seen. Whenever my mother was hanging clothes on the washline, or feeding the chickens we penned in our backyard, Walth would call out, "Pretty soon the Nancy comes from California."

One afternoon at the beginning of the summer, as I eased Grandpa into his chair outside, I saw her. There was a beach blanket spread between two lilacs in Walth's backyard. In the short grass a transistor radio, the first I'd ever heard, played "Ring of Fire" by Johnny Cash. And Nancy, in a two piece swimsuit, was wandering around the yard, a quiet smile on her moist lips, her long hair loose down her back. Under her low-cut top, I could see the valley, and then the upward slope, of her swelling breasts. Looking at her, I felt something of the unspoken things that happen between men and women: it was my first bout with love.

After a while, she lay down on her towel, closing her eyes and stretching out her long legs to the sky. I tried ignoring her. I tried to concentrate on Grandpa, wondering what his thoughts were, but his silence only made me imagine a great white blizzard blowing through his head. Maybe that was what was happening to him. Or maybe he sensed my wavering attention, for just as I stared at her more boldly, he jabbed his cane toward the heavens like he was trying to stop the sun, and said hoarsely in German, "It's not the same sun I knew."

Those were the first words he'd spoken since he'd come to stay with us, but I didn't answer; for I was embarrassed by this worn old man on a kitchen chair in the middle of our backyard, afraid of what she might think if she saw me speaking with him. Sitting up now, she looked in our direction, shaking a cigarette from her pack. When a heavy bank of clouds edged in front of the sun, Grandpa aimed his cane at the house, so I helped him inside and returned to get the chair. It was then that Nancy, who had drawn a denim jacket around herself against the chill, called out to me, with the smoke leaking from her lips, "Come over here."

That was the beginning, my crossing into Walth's backyard. "I know you don't mind if I smoke, honey," she said, and began telling me that her visit to New Odessa was only supposed to last a week; but her parents, abruptly changing their minds, had arranged to have her stay with her grandfather most of the summer. It would take that long, she said, for her parents to cool down after the last stunt she had pulled. She had been babysitting a one-year-old, she said, and wondering how it would feel, had removed her blouse and let the infant suck at her bare breast. Just then the mother had returned without warning. "And here I am in North Dakota," she said, lighting another cigarette from the butt of her first one.

The story about the baby confused and frightened me. The cigarette, the way she trailed her fingers along the inside of her tanned legs as she spoke, and the direct way she looked at me — it all made me nervous. As sunshine washed over the yard again, I hugged my knees as though it was my last hold before falling into a dark well, and she lay back on her towel like I wasn't even there.

"Come again tomorrow," she finally said.

Each afternoon I would leave Grandpa by himself and sit with her. She'd smoke and tell me about her life in California: drunk parties on the beach where she played strip poker with young crewcut men from

the nearby army base; her bizarre sophomore classmates who believed in astral projection and had
seances to try to raise Marilyn Monroe from the dead;
and often she'd speak about her father. He was a
physician who seemed to drink most of the time —
"He's a swine for the stuff," she said — and always
seemed to be railing about his own father, Walth, and
all the backward old country ways of the man.

One afternoon she showed me her tattoo.
Underneath two Band-Aids on her ankle, she showed
me the figure of a tiny hummingbird with blurring
iridescent wings. She said that on her train ride to
North Dakota, she'd met a young man who looked like
Ringo Starr from the new Beatles group. She'd been
excited by the tattoo he'd shown her. On his belly he
had an eagle, with wings spreading to his hipbones,
the clawed feet as if gripping his belly button. After
necking in the park during a layover, he had led her
to a tattoo parlor in Cheyenne, Wyoming. "But if
Walth ever sees it, I'll be dead forever," she said, making me swear I would never tell. When I agreed to ab-
solute silence, she took her inkpen and wrote my
name along the inside of her thigh, just below the
edge of her swimsuit.

I hardly said anything all those afternoons, afraid
she would laugh at me the way she did at the town:
at the tiny main street, the water tower that looked
like the tin man in the Wizard of Oz, and the crude
boys who followed her the first day in town like a pack
of wild dogs, hooting and whistling. "They act like
they never saw a girl before," she said.

Weeks passed. Lilacs and flowering crabs dropped
their blossoms. Rains rolled in from the north, followed by soft winds that blew the sweet scent of alfalfa

into town from the surrounding fields. It was the heart of summer.

I began neglecting my chores, I skipped baseball practices, I was impatient with Grandpa and my little brothers. The only thing I wanted was to spend those afternoons with her, or watch her, as I did one morning, as she wandered about Walth's yard, leaning against the columns that supported the porch, her hair loose, the wind pulling her nightgown tight around her legs, In the evenings on my bed in the basement room, I turned my face to the wall, and in the swirls of plaster found lost islands, hidden archipelagoes, knowing my own feelings frightened me, knowing that she was so different from me, with all she knew and dared.

My parents noticed the change in me; they couldn't help it. One evening at supper my father confronted me. He slammed his fist on the table until the silverware rattled, and said, "As long as you have your feet under my table, you work." The next day he was home from work early; worried, I threw myself into the chores. But he just ran a wet comb through his hair, trimmed his moustache, and as he changed to a clean, grey workshirt, I could hear him speak with my mother about our supper guests for that evening. I didn't pay much attention. At least once a month my mother invited our minister and his wife for supper; and sometimes my father brought home a linoleum salesman he met in his work at the hardware store. When my mother set the dishes on the table, I tied my little brothers into their highchairs with dish towels, and then went to get Grandpa.

"Kum herein," my mother was saying, inviting our visitors inside, and as Grandpa and I made our way through the kitchen I saw Walth, bobbing his head in apology for being late, and behind him Nancy, who was smiling strangely and nodding her head towards Grandpa's feet. Despite my help, he could only shuffle, and when I looked down and saw the throw rug from the living room bunched in front of his slippers, I hated him. I hated him for embarrassing me. I hated him too for that glassy look from a time before I was born, for all the odors of liniment and old age he carried with him, for his yellowed fingernails — everything.

My father recited the old German prayer about Jesus being our guest and sharing our food, and then as the food was being passed, Grandpa kept moving his fork over his empty plate, looking down at the rounded surface like it was an empty sun.

"Wek — gone, everything is gone," he said.

"But you haven't eaten yet, Grossvater," my mother said, cutting sausage into pieces for my little brothers to fist into their mouths; and as I did the same for Grandpa, cutting the casing on his piece, Nancy rolled her eyes up in disgust.

Finally Walth, who had been born in the same German colony in Russia as Grandpa, said, "Yah in the old country we had horses, stone houses, and it was hot enough for wine grapes. Gel? — Isn't that so?"

When Grandpa made no reply, Walth buttered a thick slice of my mother's homebaked bread, then added, "Yah the bread. Ay. We ate it at night so we wouldn't have to look at it, when we was crossing the big waters of the ocean . . . Worms."

"That's all gone," Grandpa said. "Russland. The sun. The ocean. Everyone who came."

"Yeah the worms," Walth said, smiling. "They're

gone too."

"Shpot," Grandpa said, glaring, using the dialect word that meant mockery, for he felt Walth was making fun of him.

My father quickly rose. He allowed no arguing and often no conversation at his table — "Are we eating or are we talking," he sometimes said. From the cupboard he brought a gallon of homemade chokecherry wine and poured each of the adults a glass. It wasn't long before the conversation became relaxed, shifting from English to German, and the adults, finishing their meal, wanted to be alone. Nancy and I were told to take the children into the other room and entertain them.

"Your grandpa is a crazy old fart," she said as we spilled some building blocks on the living room floor for my brothers. Even if she was right, and even if I felt the same way, I couldn't renounce Grandpa to her. I heard myself say, with my mother's emphasis in my voice, "He's just lonely. And old."

"He is still crazy," she said. "Like this piddly town."

In the kitchen Walth was talking about his granddaughter. He spoke German dialect, and my parents did too, all of them certain they were the only ones who could understand. But as I'd grown older, I'd learned to listen carefully to put words and phrases together, and the language was no longer, to me anyway, one of secrecy.

Walth was worried about Nancy. His phone lines, he said, were burning up with calls. Every night a different car came for her — loud cars with wide wheels and rough-looking young men with slicked back hair. I had heard the cars myself, been jealous listening, but each afternoon there she would be, in the backyard, waiting for me, and everything else melted away.

From where I sat in the living room, I could see Walth finishing his glass of wine. "Yah she should see a nize boy like yours," he said with finality.

Grandpa, as if in agreement, lifted his glass too, dribbling a few drops onto his lips, as he said, "Koople, koople."

Everyone laughed and started telling stories about koopling, the way their ancestors in Russia had been married: by arrangement, with parents making marriage decisions of young people. My mother said quietly that that was how her mother had married Grandpa. And when she joked with Walth that he should be koopled with a widowed cousin of hers, Grandpa said she had better hurry, and recited the old proverb, "Spring rains and old people's dances don't last long."

Then it was decided. Not a koopling. Just that I should take Nancy to the movies the coming Saturday night, since she would be leaving New Odessa the next day.

In the morning my mother told me the plans. I made a show of hesitancy, but she insisted, as I knew she would, saying we owed Mr. Walth a favor for all the times he had sharpened our knives at his millstone, and helped us with chicken butchering and potato planting. "Go," she said. "It will be good for you."

It was a long wait. Friday seemed ages away. In the middle of the week, to make things worse, it was raining and I stayed inside, helping Grandpa shuffle from room to room for his exercise. When he tired,

I played with my little brothers. I let them bang on old pots and pans, and sometimes, when thoughts of her stirred in my belly like sweet winds, I whispered into their ears, knowing my secrets were safe, "She is beautiful," or, "I love her." One afternoon as Friday drew near, I repeated shameful things to them about Nancy and me. That evening, feeling guilty, I watched them closely, fearful my dark words would somehow show in their innocent play.

Then it was Saturday evening. We met in the alley behind our homes, and together walked past the used farm equipment lot where the long necks of combines stuck out of the weeds like dinosaurs crooning at the sky. The alley led to the gravel street; there we walked past the Red Owl store, a carry-out boy trundling a metal cart heaped with grocery sacks towards large-finned cars parked at angles against the curb.

She talked most of the way, about her flight home the next day, and how much of a drag New Odessa had been all summer. Then, as we crossed the pot-holed parking lot across the street from the theater, where the marquee announced the movie *Parent Trap* with Hayley Mills, she scuffed some dirt over her cigarette butt and said, "You know, you are just like your shitty old gramps."

We sat near the back, and as the first wobbly frames appeared on the screen, I stared straight ahead, hurt, thinking maybe I was more like Grandpa than I cared to admit: repulsive to her, my worst fear, as though his old age had infected me. I felt her mohair sweater against my shoulder as her hand closed on mine, and when I didn't react, she whispered in my ear, "I mean you don't say much."

Afterwards, we walked along the two blocks of the main street, where polka music blared from the bars.

83

Farmers with white foreheads and tanned cheeks gathered in small groups on the sidewalk, talking about their balers and the thick second cut of alfalfa they'd managed midsummer.

Then we walked over the fractured and crumbling sections of old sidewalk that led past quiet homes and sprinklers pulsing on lawns. Sometimes cottonwoods and boxelders spread their branches over us. Around an occasional streetlight hordes of insects buzzed in wild funnels. Overhead, the night was a high dome of stars. As we neared our homes, she said she needed one last smoke before going inside for the night. We leaned against a rusting combine near the alley behind our homes, and when I looked over at her, all I could see was the cigarette burning between her fingers like nerve endings in the dark, and that dark web of textured nylons covering her legs.

I looked at our yards sunk in darkness, and knew it was our last time together. As I thought of that, and wondered what to say, she started telling me how every evening before bed, to add a little spice to her life, she stood naked in front of her mirror in Walth's basement and drew on herself with red lipstick. "It beats counting sheep," she said, flicking her cigarette away and walking to her door. From behind the screen door, she beckoned me close, pressing her moist lips against mine, our first kiss through Walth's rusty screen, and said, "Come to my window tonight."

Later, I lay on my bed, knowing that beyond my wall and a few feet through the earth, she was in her room, too, waiting. For a while, one of my little brothers cried, and I could hear my mother soothing him. Then, in the other bedroom upstairs, I heard Grandpa. At first, since his voice was so highpitched, I thought he was crying. As I began to understand words and phrases in German, I realized it was a prayer, a long one, for the three wives he had outlived, "now lost in the earth," he said; for his children who hadn't survived the influenza epidemic of 1918, or died later, "now hidden from the light of the sun," he said; for everyone in the farflung network of family, the aunts and great-uncles and cousins scattered across the country, "like seeds in a hard wind," he said. And he was praying for the boy — "Der Bu," as he called me — to be led to the right path, to be given strength to resist sin, to be strong in the days of his youth. When he finished, and finally breathed his amen, I could almost feel the weight of his words in the dark room above me, pressing down.

At eleven o'clock, I walked through our quiet house, crossing into Walth's yard. The night was alive with crickets, the grass damp, as I got on my hands and knees to look into her window. She stood in front of her mirror, her clothes pooled around her feet. Her shoulder blades looked like small wings buried beneath her skin. In the reflection of her mirror, I could see her breasts, and the red circles she'd drawn around them. On her belly she'd drawn a large circle around her navel, and she was filling it in with lipstick, like a child coloring. And along the inside of her legs, she had written my name, over and over, in wild, careening loops.

When she saw me, she positioned a chair beneath the window and swung the sash open from the inside. I struggled with the rusty hinges of the storm window, only that single pane of glass remaining between us, afraid neighbors might see me, or Walth might wake up. I slid through the window and onto the chair, entering the makeshift bedroom Walth had fashioned for her visit. There in the space between bedsheets draped over clothesline rope stretched between posts, on a shaky old brass bed, we were together for hours; and I learned, as many people finally learn, about that strange, sometimes shameful thing that exists in them.

Early the next morning I stood in Walth's garage. It was cool inside. Frayed fanbelts hung from sagging joists. The roof needed new shingles; lozenges of light, like a thousand suns, shone onto the oil-stained gravel where Walth usually parked his old Studebaker. I had hoped to say goodbye; but they'd left before dawn for Bismarck, where Nancy would catch her flight for California. Maybe I would write her and she'd reply, I told myself out loud. Maybe we'd see each other soon. Maybe she'd come again next summer. But my words just sounded hollow in the empty garage.

After breakfast I volunteered to stay home with Grandpa; everyone else was going to church. Before my mother left, she dressed Grandpa in a long-sleeved shirt and his old slouch cap, and warned me, "And don't let him burn out there."

In the backyard, I eased Grandpa into his chair. The dog days of August had set in; the heat rose from the earth in shimmering waves. I wanted to take off my shirt, but knew the smeared lipstick from the night before covered my chest like a wild tattoo. Tired, I lay down in the grass near his chair. For a while, I kept my eyes open. Flying grasshoppers rattled in the air around us. Grandpa stared off at the pastures beyond town, the shadows from the brim of his cap moving over his seamed, lonely face. Then I let myself drift into an uneasy sleep, hoping he would prod me with his cane when he had enough of the sun that beat down on both of us.

Sunflowers for the Assassin

I first met Tafiq in Lahore, a place he called the City of the Dead. It was in the teak-paneled den of a mansion floating in acres of landscaped lawns. There were western diplomats, many in Pakistani dress, and wealthy Pakistani industrialists sporting American leisure suits, and one man whom I thought looked like the dictator of some banana republic. Perhaps it was his bull neck; certainly it was the old Woolsey pith helmet on his head.

"General Zia is a worm," he announced. "Don't you agree?"

That was the beginning of our conversation. He told me that in the previous government he had been Minister of A--; and recenty, for illegal political activity, jail had been his home. His only current political activity, he explained, was calling the General names. He laughed then, maniacally it seemed, that laugh rising from low to high like that of a radio villain. Then, in a rather bored manner, he recited the sins of the coalition of Islamic fundamentalists and army officers, headed by this General Zia who, the year before, had seized power.

"But now," he said, "sunflowers have replaced my

political ambition."

A company, he added, in a far-off place called Fargo, North Dakota, was selling him sunflower seed. Proudly he displayed his satchel, emblazoned with the company's stickers.

"When I become prime minister," he said like he was addressing a throng, "I will pave Pakistan with sunflowers, God willing."

When I told him my home was North Dakota, his eyes lit up and his head looked as though it was about to rise off his collar. He grabbed my hand with both of his, pumping fiercely.

"Then you are my friend, Rossler," he said. "My brother."

While people around us discussed exotic vacation spots like Sri Lanka and the lakes of Kaghan Valley, Tafiq talked about North Dakota and sunflowers.

"With all those sunflowers," he said, "your state must be a paradise."

"Yes," I said, "but a frozen one."

We parted fast friends, and over the next six months my association with Tafiq became well-known. But so much occurred I hardly had time to reflect on the warnings I'd received about him. Many said his ambition was insatiable; others knew him as a con artist, working the black market with consummate skill; the dictator felt Tafiq was a dangerous political agitator.

That next winter I accepted an invitation to visit his family and found myself in his Datsun, heading towards Pakistan's border with Afghanistan. The crate in the back seat, he said, contained oranges.

"Gifts for my family," he said with a shifty smile, but I knew better.

We'd left Lahore in the early morning, with the turnip-shaped domes and the ancient walls of Akbar rising from the haze, and drove into the open country. Wrecked vehicles littered the ditches, and Tafiq pointed them out to me with a kind of glee I didn't care for. Buses and trucks raced by, blaring streaks of sound, reminding me there are few rules on Pakistani roads. Tafiq reminded me too, leaning on the accelerator like he was trying to drive into the future. It was late winter and cool; but I was sweating and holding on.

Farmland poured by, wheat I thought; strings of heavily-laden donkeys became a blur. Tafiq was a good driver, too good, with fine-toned reflexes that liked to be tested, and an instinct for open space — something we needed, for the traffic was heavy, the road narrow and in bad repair, thick with animal herds and lackadaisical pedestrians.

"I drive fast," Tafiq said, "so if we have an accident we die quickly. There are no hospitals here. Dogs would lick our blood."

I shuddered; he threw his head back in laughter, dark laughter, while our car narrowly missed a stalled bus. Every time the car veered, those oranges in the back seat clanked in their crates.

"Your relatives must have strong teeth," I teased.

"They are a more exotic fruit than oranges," he answered. "Given the times."

Given the times, I thought, could mean only one thing. It had been just four months since the Russians marched into Afghanistan. He'd slowed down some now, but I was still sweating, from a different kind of fear this time.

Driving seemed to free him. He began to talk more

than I'd ever heard him, voluminously, but always in loops that led back to his own political hopes and the hopes for Pakistan which he'd erected around the ideas of the German philosopher Oswald Spengler.

"We are a decadent civilization," Tafiq explained. "You Americans are now on top. But we will get off our dead asses, and if you leave us alone in the right ways, we rise, you fall — and the new Asiatic civilization Spengler envisioned will come to be."

There was an element of strangeness as we drove through alluvial lowlands drained by the five rivers of the Punjab, with Tafiq reciting from memory pages of the man's writing. We drove all day — past towns founded in prehistory by snake worshippers and places destroyed by the Mongols. The headlights poured into the darkness, illuminating caravans of tattooed camels and spectral acacia shrub. Tafiq looked tired, so I offered to drive.

"You wouldn't kill us, Rossler," he said. "You would drive too slowly, with your western concern for safety. I have no desire to wave my stumps in the market for money."

That wild laughter came again, rising up to places I didn't care to venture.

"That is the difference between us," he said. "It matters to you that you live. For me life is different — ten years, ten minutes, all the same."

We stayed the night in his private suite in the Intercontinental Hotel in Islamabad. In the morning we surveyed the American Embassy. Several Americans had been killed there, and the staff nearly burned alive. The windows of all the buildings were glassless, the interiors charred, the grounds as deserted as an ancient excavated city — it was the fruit of November,

1979. The hostages had been taken in Iran, and the Muslim world was alive with rumors that Americans had attacked the holy city of Mecca. Thinking back six months to that time, I knew I owed a lot to Tafiq. Mostly my life, several times over. When a mob attacked the Lahore consulate, it was Tafiq who hid me in his car. There were shouts, the hail of bricks, the rushes of heat from cars bursting into flames, gunshots. But even Tafiq couldn't get me and my family out of the country. He hid us for a week, and when we returned home, my cook told me he'd heard rumors the house was going to be firebombed. It was a hopeless, sinking feeling, like being lost in a blizzard. Meanwhile, Tafiq had left town. On the roof of my house I stood watch, two days without sleep, waiting, and once I fell asleep for an instant, dreaming fitfully of a howitzer on the roof, covering the gate. That dream was all I had for protection until Tafiq arrived. He sat in a chair by the front window, sweating yet refusing to remove the long overcoat he'd arrived in.

"My arsenal," he said, patting his bulky midsection, "might frighten your boy."

He loved boys, of course. His favorite saying was "baby is king." He was the oldest son in a culture that revered males. By his own admission he was pampered and spoiled. But he sat there for three days solid, shouting to my cook for more food, more beer. Surrounded by empty bottles, he looked like some grotesque pigeon caught in its own droppings.

We had talked about how, after all this trouble, I would accompany him to his own village, how maybe we would hunt boar together at Jhelum. Later he would visit me in North Dakota. Once he hollered for more beer, and when my cook didn't appear immediately he said, "You must train these squashed cabbage leaves you call servants. Give them your boot. Oh, but I forget — you Americans have such odd ideas about equality."

"Small mobs I take care of," he said. "Big mobs, you run into the graveyard. I have made plans for you from there. Other than that, my hands are cut off in this matter."

No sooner had he spoken than he was out the door, coattails flying, something bright flashing between the leaves of the hedge. I could hear him at the gate, shouting to a group of people on motorcycles.

"Cross over this line," he said in Urdu, "and I shoot."

Then they were gone. The air filled with the whine of motorcycles, gears punished to build up speed.

Yes, I thought now, leaving Islamabad and heading for his home in the mountains, I owed a lot to him. That crate was still in the back seat, and there was another day of driving, of bad roads (two flats, a broken steering column), of men along the road cracking brick with little hammers. But there were mountains now, heaped along the horizon like someone's forgotten promises.

At Peshawar, near the border, men milled around with bandoliers and guns and hatred for Russians. Tafiq left me with a cousin of his in a copper bazaar, casually mentioning before he left that I was not a captured Russian. Several hours later he returned, driving a Suzuki pickup with plastic flowers from a wedding celebration twined around the wipers. There were four crates in back now, not one.

"That's a lot of oranges," I said, trying to pry loose

the secret.

"I have a lot of relatives," he said.

Narrow roads took us far into the provinces where fan-shaped talus piles spilled down over-grazed slopes and terraces of farmland lay like patchwork around the mountains. But these were only foothills; in the distance were the real mountains, the Himalayas — rising to the heart of Asia, the rooftop of the world. Along the road now, camped around small fires, were people in rough, dark clothing — Afghan refugees.

Tafiq's village was what I expected — mud-walled, wooden doors chiseled with floral designs, naked kids playing between the legs of animals. His relatives were strong, open-faced people who greeted us warmly. But before I knew it, those crates were unloaded and out of sight.

There was no electricity. We sat under a crescent of stars while darkness like that left over from the first night of the world spread around us. Sugary tea was served, but I couldn't be too careful. Tafiq heard me drop the water purification tablet into my cup.

"No germs in the mountains, Rossler," he said. "Only Russians." That laugh again; rising, like it was scaling those mountains in the dark. Something was eating at him, something big.

I slept badly, explosions resounding between the morning and my dreams. I awoke to Tafiq sticking his head into the open doorway. Behind him the pines were rising towards the sun like iron filings. I could still hear the far-away concussions.

"The graveyard shift," he said, like he was reading my thoughts. "Blasting for minerals."

After breakfast, some men made preparations for a journey. The older men had sten guns; the younger ones shouldered the Russian AK-47's, and the rifles seemed unfamiliar to them. Tafiq started to explain to me that each family along the border sends one man to fight the Russians, an obligation to their brothers in Afghanistan. Just then it occurred to me that those rifles had been the oranges in the back seat, and when I looked at Tafiq his mouth was pulled into the rictus of a smile.

All the while I'd assumed I'd accompany them. Now Tafiq motioned for me to remain.

"How would we explain a dead American?" he shouted back.

I stayed in the village. It was harvest time, so I worked out in the fields with veiled women and half-naked men, hacking at wheat with a curved knife that was crying for a sharp edge. A long drink from a brass tureen put me on my back for three days, and I stared at the ceiling and thought about the rifles, the AK-47's. I remembered hearing rumors that Sadat in Egypt had weapons of Russian make left over from the time before he'd expelled the Russians from his country. The CIA, with help from men like Tafiq, was funneling the weapons through Pakistan to the rebels.

Tafiq returned a week later. He was haggard, but walking like he couldn't believe there was still earth beneath his feet. When he saw me he dropped into a crouch, his hands vibrating in front of him. One of his cousins cut at the air with his hands, saying "bomba, bomba." Not all of them came back, but I didn't ask any questions. The next day, we headed back to Lahore. Our wheels skirted mountain ledges. There were a dozen near collisions, and my arm jerked to my face, a hopeless reflex. The roads were just as narrow and clogged. Tafiq was just as oblivious; quoting his Spengler, drifting in memories, driving fast.

On the Fourth of July a party was held at the consul-general's mansion. I hadn't seen Tafiq for months. Rumors were he was receiving CIA training. Newspapers maintained he was trying to revive the banned People's Party. Servants in damp uniforms were hefting cases of beer through the front gate. I followed them, knowing I would find the beer tub, and, if he was anywhere in the subcontinent, Tafiq. I looked around for the pith helmet, the well-tailored flannel suit he favored. All I saw were the usual Americans. One man — in star-spangled tennis shoes and Bermudas — was bent over the galvanized tub, throwing aside beer and ice chunks.

"This is an American holiday," the man shouted. "Why do you have cheap beer that gives hangovers? Where is your good American beer? I think you are a tired people who dress like clowns. A few helicopters crash in the desert and you forget how to celebrate. You will probably have German sausage for lunch, not hot dogs."

It was Tafiq. When he saw me, he shouted, "They have told me not to attend these functions anymore. So I have disguised myself, as an American." He indicated his clothing.

"My friend," he said. "I have just returned from your North Dakota. Your gentle mother sends her greetings. Unfortunately the sunflowers were not in bloom during my stay there."

We went through the archway of a hedge to a parking lot behind the mansion, where we sat on the back steps, sipping beer. In the parking lot, parked bumper to bumper, were the vehicles burned in November. The evening call to prayer came from a nearby mosque. Servants lit the smudge torches lining the driveway, and the cars set on their rims made silhouettes that looked like sinking ships.

"I will never see those sunflower fields in bloom," he said.

He started talking about his hopes for Pakistan. His voice, usually so resonant, had a bitter quality to it now. I could feel him getting worked up about the General again, so I tried to change the subject.

"You look like our friend Oswald," I said, referring to the philosopher, Spengler, whose photograph I'd seen on the flyleaf of a book. There was a strong resemblance I felt — same muscular neck, the lobed forehead, and intensity welding the features. Tafiq looked pained at what I'd said, infinitely so.

"You will be silent," he said weakly, "about this thing."

I didn't understand. He stood, his shoulders blotting the light in the archway like an eclipse.

"Remember,'" he said, walking away. "You are my friend, my brother."

I walked to the front gate and out into the street, letting the noise of the traffic pass into the breach that had opened between us.

Unexpectedly I had to leave the country. Over the Arabian Sea, I remembered I hadn't even said good-bye to Tafiq. There was a stop in Dubai — that purgatory of sheiks in white robes — then through London and home. Pakistan seemed so far away, with so little in common with this, my other life in North Dakota. Often, I'd wonder about Tafiq.

One evening not long ago I was driving through

the county where I grew up. The fields of sunflowers on the glacial hills rolled away from both sides of the road to infinity it seemed, and I remembered Tafiq's favorite quote from Spengler, something about regarding the flowers, how they closed in the evening sun, about the fear one felt in the presence of this earth-bound existence.

Later, a small newspaper article drew my attention. There had been an attempt on the life of the Pakistani dictator. The would-be assassin had been killed. A brief report, nothing more.

It came to me again, that pain on Tafiq's face the last time I'd seen him. I had said he looked like Oswald. I had meant the German philosopher. But, overestimating the parallels of our thoughts, I used only the man's first name. Tafiq had misunderstood. It became clear now: he thought I had said he looked like Lee Harvey Oswald, Kennedy's assassin.

That evening the phone rang — a call I knew was coming. A bad connection; distance thinning the voice to a barely audible whisper. I could make out enough to confirm what I already knew: Tafiq was dead in that City of the Dead, Lahore. And it all had something to do with flowers, I thought, closing in the setting sun, with fields of sunflowers waiting to be harvested, or harvested now.

97

Stones

hose last years Grandma rarely spoke, and if she did, it was in German, with people long dead and gone from the earth. She no longer recognized me; and more hurt than sympathetic, I avoided visiting her. But things changed, or I changed, and sometime after my own son was born, when my own place in the generations became clearer, I knew it was important to see her again.

So one clear Sunday afternoon in July, a day too beautiful to be spent indoors, with her metal walker in my backseat and my two year old strapped between us, and with Grandma nodding towards the New Odessa Rest Home and saying angrily, "Nothing but old people in there" — we started on our journey.

The gravel road slanted south of town, and we drove past a gravel pit and then the city cemetery, where on a low hill the tombstones stuck up like thumbs. "And dead ones in there," she said, turning her face away. When we turned onto the highway, with cars and pickups passing us in random gusts, she asked again where it was we were going, and I told her, "Where you once lived."

Where you were once happy, I almost said, for I

99

knew that if she had ever been happy it was on that farm with her first husband Willie. But he had died, half a century ago now, leaving her with three small children. Even now nurses at the rest home told me she sometimes cried, wondering who was caring for them, her babies.

At the six mile curve, with the air sweet from mown alfalfa, and bales scattered toward the horizon, I couldn't help but remember the springtimes of my adolescence. Weekends I had worked for farmers, loading rocks onto what we called a stoneboat, an iron slab hitched by chains to a sun-bleached tractor. And it was always a revelation to me then that the following spring — since frost had forced them to the surface — rocks again covered the fields. They were, I decided, earth's unseen, steady crop. As we drove, I could see along the fence lines piles of rocks gathered by so many hands over so many years; cairns of labor. And beyond those rocks and fences I knew were the road drainage channels, the blue skins of glacially formed lakes, and the rolling cropland. It was home, a beautiful county, once you saw past the work.

I felt similarly ambivalent about Grandma. Now, as she sat quietly in my car, it was hard to believe she had so often burdened our family with her difficulties and her incessant fights with her second husband. And she had often harangued my parents on religious matters, warning them that if any of us children died, we would burn forever, because we hadn't been baptised correctly. These arguments belonged to another age, just as Grandma herself seemed a refugee from some lost time and that village near the Black Sea where she had been born.

She had chanted healing rhymes in dialect over

my childhood hurts, rhymes I repeated now with my own child. And she hated the Catholics with a fervor that seemed medieval, her hate aimed at their incomprehensible, robe-wearing and inflammatory ways; who was it, she would ask, that sang so loudly on Sundays, trying to drown out the hymns we raised to the Lord's glory in our evangelical church a block away? She feared crawling things, "grottla," she called them: the snakes she chopped with her hoe, and the salamanders she had me throw into the flames of our garbage can, for she would not deign to touch their poisonous bodies. "Fire is their door into the world," she would say, "and out again too."

But her greatest fear was of the world ending. This idea so possessed her once when I was five years old — when I was already imbued with my own particulars of guilt and wrongdoing from thunderous Sunday sermons — that she came running across the street to our house, her bowlegs cutting wild arcs beneath her dress. She shouted that the harvest moon on the horizon was blood as prophesied in Revelation. Then she lifted her apron and flapped it at me as if it were another tongue, sending me to scan the sky east of town for angels blowing their horns to announce the final resurrection, and search the pastures for that last refuge of the damned — some shimmering Ararat she said lay beyond the stockyard pens.

That was long ago; but as the highway took us through the heart of the county--crossing an old wagon trail used to supply Fort Yates in frontier days, and a buffalo path where the prairie still showed corrugations from their hooves, and past pastures where cows grazed among effigies of birds and turtles and teepee rings formed by the Indians--I knew I had spent too much of my life blaming her. Just as my mother blamed Grandma for frightening me away from the church and orthodox beliefs--"You weren't raised *that* way," my mother said about my dogged refusals to attend worship services--I had always held it against Grandma for teaching me that only decay and confusion lay at the root of life.

My son, who was all fists and diapers then, with moods and tantrums that too often matched my own, started crying and continued for miles. Finally Grandma looked over at me and said angrily that the child must be a girl, with such red cheeks--"die rota backa," she said--and such a high voice. When I stopped to change his diaper in the backseat, for that was why he was so irascible, I asked Grandma in German if she wanted to find out for certain if he really was a girl; but she just looked away, saying, "Ach, I think you are the one acting like a girl now, changing that diaper."

My intentions were lighthearted, and I was reminded of the times when I used to visit her, when she no longer knew who I was, and she would display the humor so characteristic of the Black Sea Germans, those immigrants to America from colonies in Czarist Russia. Once, when she saw my cut-offs and shoulder-length hair, she said I was too long on one end and too short on the other. Another time I found her sitting in the waning moments of daylight, and we talked in German dialect about an old Norwegian farmhand she'd once cooked for, and laughed together about how when he wanted dessert after a full meal he would call out to her, "What's for pie?" The same evening I had asked her about a bruise on her forehead, and with her thoughts bending to earlier times, she'd replied, "Those damn cows, you *know* how they kick the pails when you milk."

Grandma's second marriage, arranged through a koopelsman or matchmaker in the old country fashion, led to despair for both of them. My mother wrote me in my junior year of college that Grandma's second husband, a quiet man who took to alcohol, had died of a broken heart. "He was buried on a cold day last week," she wrote. "Now both of them have some peace I think."

But there wasn't to be much peace for Grandma. Refusing to cook any longer, she moved against her will into the retirement home; one hot summer day, wrapped in a long winter coat, she walked across town like an avenging angel to confront my mother: "What do I want in there with all those old people?" she said.

Halfway to the farm now we passed one of those abandoned two-story farmhouses so common in the county--an empty yard, scraps of curtains flapping in dormer windows, and a few outbuildings leaning their unpainted shapes into the wind. The desolation reminded me of the day in the county courthouse when in a bound book of death certificates, I read of those who had met their ends in the county.

There were unnamed babies whose cause of death was given by the initials S.B.--which meant stillborn. The loss of one child was "due to runaway horses." Convulsions and hemorrhages, hypertension or "old age' — I read until the dead seemed to outnumber the living and the county seemed a charnel house. And there were the recordings in the weary hand of the county coroner Dr. Grant, of eight children from the same family, dead from Spanish influenza in 1918, during an epidemic that Grandma called in dialect "die sinflut," or The Deluge.

That time was long past too. Sometimes I can hear family voices, and who can blame them, saying, "Forget the dead, they're gone." But Grandma could never forget; she still carried that pain. Once when my younger brother had a rash and severe fever, Grandma was summoned. She felt his hot forehead, then jerked her hand away and hurried out the door, her voice rising to a quavery pitch of fear, saying it was the dreaded scarlet fever. It wasn't, but that is how it was with those early times and that old fear, working to the surface like those stones in the field.

With my son playing quietly with some magnetic alphabet letters and Grandma staring at fields of wheat and barley turning golden brown at their roots, the time passed quickly and it wasn't long before we arrived. As we neared the farm, the long grass brushed against the chassis and I could see at intervals pink quartzite markers--as tall as I am--lining the border with South Dakota; this was the farthest edge of my childhood world, a place I had heard Grandma talk about with such frequency and emotion, about Willie and her children, that it had assumed almost mythical proportions in my thoughts. But the only real evidence of life now was a long line of cottonwoods and some elms, old ones planted at the turn of the century, that wrapped around most of the farmstead like a green arm. The crumbled-in foundation where the small house once stood, and the lines of fieldstones that had once supported a small granary, and the tired looking barn sagging in on itself--that all made the place seem barren.

My son wandered off, chasing flying grasshoppers

between an abandoned hayrake and a pile of rotting lumber. Grandma, who seemed confused, just kept walking around where the house had been, sometimes peering in at the crumbled cement and buckling walls that had once been her basement, or nudging with her shoe at wrappings of baler twine, empty grease cylinders, and crushed beer cans left behind from an adolescent party.

With the wind high in the cottonwoods, bending their tops, and goldfinches and swallows riding the sideways currents of air around us, I stood there remembering Grandma's children. There was my step-father, a sad stoop-shouldered man whom I came to know when I was about the same age as my son now; but he had died young. There was Aunt Norene, who returned from her home in California every few years to visit, sporting garish earrings ("Now you look like a gypsy," Grandma told her once) and blood-red fingernails, and a travelling decanter for vodka in her suitcase. She would hug and kiss everyone, leaving relatives recoiling--for emotion of that kind was better reserved for the mid-week prayer meetings in our evangelical church, when people delivered out loud what seemed like endless German prayers of self-castigation. And each time Norene kissed Grandma on the cheek, Grandma reacted: first with anger, then with chagrin and embarrassment--but always saying, "That was a Judas kiss."

Norene eventually died as well. Later, when it was learned that she had been cremated, a relative confided in me, in a sad pronouncement concerning the breakdown of family ties and the passing of an old way of life: "Your Aunt Norene was burned like an animal, without services or words said over her." That left only the youngest of Grandma's offspring alive, an uncle in a nearby town. The last I had seen of him he looked in pain, a kind of self-absorbed suffering, as he saw his entire generation slipping away, drawing him in the same direction.

Grandma stood beside me now. Despite the heat and as though to protect herself, she gathered her sweater around herself; she seemed ready to leave. My son, whose grasshopper hunt had been unsuccessful, was thirsty and restless, wrapping himself around one of my legs. And I felt as those in their middle years must always feel, leaned on by both the past and future; so with the sun still high, we started back.

The washboard road made the car shake, gravel stones knocked against the oil pan, and my child began to cry until we reached the smooth two-lane highway. Then there was only the wide land and the long lines of shelter belts pivoting about us as we drove, and he finally slept. The rest of the way back Grandma talked of all the work she'd done that morning, and how much worry--"viela sorga"--it brought her to work in the barn with no one watching her children. Agitated, she started to pick at the lint of her sweater. And it must have been with the same tenacity, I thought, that she cleared rocks or gathered buffalo bones, cooked for a summer kitchen of threshers or done all the countless chores that constituted her life then. But her existence seemed so narrow, now that I felt remorse to think of it.

Back in the New Odessa Rest Home, she pushed her guest book toward me, wanting my name. "Such a nice man," she said, who'd driven her that long distance--"da driva," she kept saying. "Over there." While I signed under her watchful eye, for she'd forgotten I had already written my name twice on my arrival, my boy tottered into the hallway. There were old women out there mostly, bent over canes and walkers and slumped in wheelchairs, calling to him in German with tremulous voices: "Come, come." They asked his name as he sat in their laps, asked if he was a boy or girl, and told him what a fine child he was.

When it was time to go, I kissed Grandma on the cheek, the most affectionate gesture I had ever offered her. As I left her room, and as the old women in the hallway were holding out their arms for my son to give them a goodbye hug, I could hear Grandma saying to herself, "Judas kiss--that was a Judas kiss."

That evening I drove around town to put my child to sleep. He was protesting, toys went flying, nothing was good enough--it had been a long day in a strange place for him. I drove past our old house, and across the street from it saw Grandma's: abandoned and in bad repair, with planks missing from the steps, and the washline sagging and the posts leaning badly. My son's whimpering was steady and knowing he was on the verge of sleep, I headed north of town. I drove past the blacksmith's shop, remembering that as a child I watched sparks dance inside and thought the blacksmith in his metal mask was a wizard calling upon some dark prairie powers to repair the broken discs and plows and bicycles that littered his shop. Then, with pigeons swooping low for grain spilled along the tracks, I drove past the grain elevator, so much smaller than I remembered it, at its top the single window that Grandma always told me was God's Eye, holy and judging and forever watching me and my sins. Easing the car over the edges of the metal rails of the Soo Line, I could see the shining tracks curving and lifting in the distance, like a hoop around the northern edge of New Odessa.

Out in the country darkness was falling over the boulder strewn hills. The sun was setting. In the distance a doe went over a fence with a fluid kick. By the time I turned the car around my child was asleep.

On my way back to town, passing the sloping pastures and fields of alfalfa and summer fallow, I kept telling myself that it wasn't a Judas kiss I'd given Grandma--that deep in the earth, though I couldn't see them, were stones, wedging towards sunlight.

Asylum

hey were brothers, twins, the same shrunken shapes moulded around a shared memory. Their large, bald heads nodded with age. Their backs curved in the same arc as their favorite wicker chairs. Inside their loose lips were pink, rabbit-like tongues and toothless gums; deep beneath hairless brows were shiny blue eyes, lost suns in the darkness of these corridors, this madhouse, home.

Lyman was the troubled one, always peering into the gloom, his mind filled with relentless questions suckled by the shadows of this place; how had they, the two boys licking at sugar cones of iced vanilla, left the white pebbled path, strayed, become lost in the waning light of a forest echoing with their parents' warnings—come straight home, watch out for the Witch? And how had they come, he wondered, to these damp tunnels, forfeiting bright summer clothes for grey uniforms, sinewy young bodies for such time-worn husks?

Corbel, his fingers tucked safely in his brother's gentle grasp, knew only of a worn promise. His face, untroubled, was glazed with anticipation. Deep wrinkles spanned from his eyes like the light from beacons set in a sea of night. He knew nothing of the questions, the trouble.

This day, this Friday, the twins shuffled through the tunnel leading from their ward. Lyman's legs were tired and heavy. Again today he had done Corbel's share of the work, sorting all of the silverware in the steamy kitchen, carrying and cleaning the heavy wooden trays while Corbel, anxious to begin the journey they took every Friday, tugged at his sleeve.

When they passed under a bare light bulb Lyman winced at the shadows smeared over the paint-peeling walls, dirty shapes that stretched into deformed fingers, like the ones that stole tokens, and fear bloomed deep within him — better that only he, Lyman, remembered those fingers, he thought. Better that he remembered for both of them. Let Corbel carry the dream and be happy.

Corbel's frail ankles and splayed out feet were bare in his ward slippers; his pants hung loosely on the bony crests of his hips--looking at his brother, Lyman realized he had again forgotten to help him dress that morning, then reprimanded himself sternly, with halting words that were not his: "Take care of Corbel. He's your brother." Corbel, hearing his name, boomed: "Yah, me Corbel," and his voice sounded down the long corridors where it was swallowed by the distance and dimness ahead.

Corbel, suddenly withdrawing his hand from his brother's, pointed at Lyman's pocket. Lyman shook his head, but when he saw the brimming tears in his brother's eyes, he reluctantly dug a smooth metal token from his pocket and pressed it into the warm folds of Corbel's outstretched hand. It was Corbel's share of the pay they had received that morning, Friday morning, for the week of work in the dishwashing room, and after Corbel brightened and handed the token back to Lyman, they linked hands and shuffled on.

Soon the tunnel divided. Lyman stopped by the mouth of the darkest branch, fixing his weak eyes on the blur of walls and grey floors ahead. He could hear her, he thought, ahead of them somewhere, clawing angrily at the walls, her hiss shivering the black silence.

"The Whi. . .the. . .Whi. . .the Whiittch," Lyman sputtered. He danced up and down, flailing his arms to block Corbel's path, but Corbel, head down, plodded obliviously forward. Lyman wrung his hands in indecision while Corbel shambled around the next corner, out of sight, then he quickly followed, pushing his hands against his upper thighs, forcing his legs to move faster, fear pounding in his veins when he heard Corbel's squeal. Turning the corner, he found Corbel cowering, arms raised as if to ward off blows. It was the Witch, moving towards them, her fisted hands spinning angrily. The twins clutched each other in terror, cringing as she danced around them. They stretched their empty hands to her, but her face glowed with rage when she saw their denial. She clamped her fingers around their bony wrists, pulling them close to the charred flesh beneath her eyes, into the foul ring of her breath. She hissed, drops of her spittle flecking their blanched faces. Her tongue snaked greedily towards them, her palms cupped as if she were holding their warm hearts, ready to squeeze the last gush of life from them. Lyman, seeing only the reflection of his own fear, dilated and huge, moving across his brother's face like a cloud, dug the tokens

111

out of his pocket and the Witch snatched them, scuttling away as she had every other Friday, with their tokens, with their hope.

Shoulders bowed with disappointment, the twins made their way back. Corbel sobbed for a moment but soon forgot, and then there was just the tired rasp of their slippers on the cold cement and Lyman's sighing as they linked hands and their grey shapes faded into the seeping shadows of the tunnel leading back to their ward.

Time passed, another week of work in the kitchen, and then again it was Friday, the day winding its way deep into their memories like these tunnels, with many abrupt ends and diverging paths, into the maze of their childhoods. They had been walking for a long time now and had come to unfamiliar surroundings. The walls were pale green and the ceilings lower. Ahead the angles and corners blurred from grey to black, darker than they had ever been, Lyman thought.

She had never waited this long before. Lyman peered forward, cocking his head cautiously, like an animal catching a scent in the wind. There were violent smears of sleeplessness beneath his eyes, for the Witch had been much in his thoughts lately. He could hear nothing, only a leaden silence flowed sluggishly through the corridors, pulling them forward, towards her huddled somewhere in the crouching dark, ready to flap and whirl around them, hungry for their fears and tokens. Oh the way, Lyman thought, would they ever find the right way.

Corbel had not asked to hold the tokens for a long time, and from the way his arms hung heavily at his sides, Lyman knew disappointment was growing in him, and jingled the tokens in his pocket. Corbel, hearing the sound, gripped Lyman's hand tightly and their faces split in sunken smiles. Hope scurried in Lyman like a quick mouse. If only they could find ice cream today. Today he, Lyman, would not give the tokens to the Witch. Yes, today, he decided, he would fight so Corbel his brother could have the ice cream.

When they came to a sign painted on the tunnel wall, PATIENTS STORE AHEAD, Lyman knew only questions. Why were there two words this time and why were the words a different color? Why were the walls closer together? Had they taken a wrong tunnel and would they now walk on forever, lost, like in the forest, night coming and the darkness closing around them like an angry hand? They should have stayed on the ward, Lyman thought, in their wicker chairs by the radiator's nest of heat, watching the bobbing heads of the sleeping others. Why had they left the ward, scuffled off the path into the unknown, looking for something they'd never find?

Corbel was walking ahead, his steps lengthening, his pale forehead shining with the memory, ice cream. With each step Lyman sank deeper and deeper into uncertainty and fear and he soon fell behind, stopping to rest in the pooled dark of a corner while Corbel waited impatiently nearby. Then there was a rattling of breath, and dry lungs scraping for air, and beside him in the corner Lyman saw a huddled heap of rags with fingers tangled harmlessly in the dirty folds, angular arms collapsed around a carbuncular face-- the Witch. The twins looked at her in disbelief. Lyman

113

shouted, shook his fist at her as if trying to rekindle the flame in her chalky cheeks, but she was drained of anger, used up, lost, mute, here in the tunnels she had haunted almost forever.

The path was clear. Nothing lay between them and the store and the ice cream. They stared at her for a long time, then linked hands and walked on, jerking their heads around to see if she followed, but she did not move. Lyman knew something of what he had seen in her face. The same feeling had often gnawed at him, the same weight, the pinched wisdom of this twilight. And he knew then, realized then, that his fear was not of the Witch; it belonged to these tunnels, seeping inside the walls like the dampness, and now it had finally felled even her.

But she was behind them and today they would find the store. Corbel slammed his flat hands together and shouted, "ice cream," his voice reaching down the tunnel and returning to them in an echo that was strong and loud. Then it wasn't long before they came to a door of smoky glass with the same sign, PA-TIENTS STORE, spelled across it. Corbel, his slack features suffused with happiness, leaned close, his tongue washing over his lips like a waterfall as he lick-ed at the letters and said, "ice cream." Easing him back, Lyman turned the knob, and together they entered.

Tokens as shiny as new moons, burnished tokens jingling and sliding across a glass counter--everywhere Corbel looked were tokens. He pushed his way through lines of grey-clad people, followed closely by Lyman. They worked their way to the counter where Corbel shouted, "ice cream." His sunken chest heav-ed with anticipation; a thin rope of saliva hung from his lower lip. Lyman pushed the two tokens across the counter to the kindly-faced woman, then turned away and looked at her once again. The outline of her face dropped into his memory, a smooth pebble that left no ripples. She wasn't the same as last time. Anxiety fluttered around his heart. The counter was different too; it had been wood, higher, their hands had strained to reach the ice cream cones.

Lyman closed his eyes, winking his brother's image into his mind, and knew Corbel was different too, different than last time, the time they had gotten ice cream, the same and yet different, and his thoughts were as confused and tangled as the tunnels. The woman pushed the tokens back. "I'm sorry," she said. "We don't have ice cream. We haven't had it any of the years I've worked here." When she saw their foreheads knot in pain, she added, "But maybe you want pop or some candy," pointing to rows of candy bars lining the shelves behind her and a large red machine near the door. Her words mixed them up and they stood for a long time staring emptily at the glass counter.

Finally, they trudged out of the store and followed the tunnel back to where it branched. Corbel was sobbing so Lyman took him by the hand and they moved along the nearest corridor, both quickly out of breath and tired; the air surrendered its chill and heat radiated from the walls, ripening large rings of sweat on their grey shirts. The tunnels began to wander and wind, veering to the right, then jogging back to the left, like the tail of some great dragon, Lyman thought, and he wondered if they had been swallowed while they slept, and maybe that was how they had come here, why they wandered and were lost.

The floor did not feel right beneath their feet and Lyman soon realized the tunnel was rising, sloping upwards, taking them with.

Ahead and above them a light played along the walls, melting shadows and dusk, scouring a yellow path on the worn cement. When the floor leveled again, they could see that the light came from a door at the end of the tunnel. Each few steps Corbel stopped, weeping inconsolably, his arms limp at his sides, withered vines in need of sun. The disappointment was scored deep in his cheeks and shards of broken dream filled his eyes. He beat his flat hands angrily at the light that bathed them as they approached the door, but Lyman led him patiently on.

They opened the door, emerging from the tunnels, eyes half closed against the brightness streaming down on them as they moved along the trembling ledges of childhood. Before them was a huge dappled expanse of green, ringed by brown-brick buildings higher than any walls they had ever seen. When something soft and invisible cooled their faces, Lyman's mouth moved gently with the word, wind. Corbel pointed to a great ball set far away in the ceiling of this blue tunnel curving above them, and in a voice clean with hope whispered, "ice cream?" "Yah, ice cream," Lyman said, gripping his brother's hand, knowing that for now, the forest, the Witch, the darkness was behind them. Together they lifted their heads and let the yellow light pour into their eyes.

Lilacs For The Czar

L ate that first night, when Joey awoke frightened from dreams of ocean waves battering his new stepfather's car, and heard in the bedroom below his own, his new grandmother talking about that day long ago when the Czar travelled through her German village on the Black Sea, heard her voice sounding young and strong and filling the room--he got out of bed and made his way down the painted stairs, tiptoeing to her room, worried and missing his mother.

He missed his mother badly, had never been away from her for even one night, and was not used to sleeping alone, as he was now in the wide brass bed upstairs, and now, now he was alone in this big house with this old woman, "your new grandmother," his mother had kept telling him, and he had wondered how anyone so ancient and creaky could ever be called new, this old woman whose voice was filling her bedroom as she talked in the middle of the night about times long ago.

But things were never what they seemed at this Grandma's, Joey thought as he stood in the hallway, listening at her door. No, he had learned that lesson the first day: that flowers weren't flowers at all, but bluma, that trees were bauma, and that the snakes in her garden (harmless creatures that his mother allowed him to handle) were poisonous schlanga and had to be chopped into pieces by her hoe.

He listened at her door, heard her talking about six horses, "milk-white horses pulling that shiny carriage," and how everyone that day of the Czar's visit had thrown flower petals at the leader, and waved and lined up in the tiny village anxious to get a glimpse of the Czar of all the Russias, and how she, as a little girl — "so eina glana madel," as she put it — was scared of the uniform and the moustaches he wore, that she ran away frightened, "just like a rabbit."

Her voice was so loud and full of energy that at first he wondered if it even was her in the bedroom, and if he should, as his mother had told him, get some help from the neighbor, Hilma Zimmerman, that sometimes Grandma didn't sleep at nights.

"Haas — tha's my name, Grandma Haas, and that means rabbit in German," she was saying, "and my Willie, when he was alive, he chased me for eleven kids across the acres of this very bed here — ho ..."

Then there was stamping and thumping and the sound of her hand slamming flat on the bed, and as Joey knocked quietly and opened the door, he could hear her saying something about rabbits, rabbits, and then all the thumping stopped as he came into the room, and only Grandma remained, sitting on the edge of her bed in a nightgown that showed the wrinkled skin of her neck.

"What's the matter? Can't sleep? Nit schlofa?" she asked.

"No," Joey said.

"What is it, I wonder, that is digging into your sleep and chewing your days into stumps — oih veh? But this old Grandma Rabbit knows. Her long ears can hear everything a boy thinks and worries — your Momma she'll come back quick, so schnell, off to bett with you, gesch!"

With those words she chased him off to bed again, and as he went back upstairs and lay in the dark on the wide brass bed, he wondered just what his mother could be doing on a honeymoon, even if it was with Grandma's son, his new stepfather. He began to whimper into his pillow, trying to cry himself to sleep; but all he could think of was his mother, and it was like the dark was pressing the worrying thoughts into his mind, and he remembered how at home he always was allowed to sleep with his light on when he was scared; but earlier in the night, he'd tried that, and his grandmother had come up the stairs and turned it off without even checking him, saying, "Burning up all the daylight again..."

But now, as he lay in bed whimpering, he heard from the bedroom below, her voice again, only talking directly to him, he thought, for who else would she be talking to in this house, unless it was that picture of the Czar she kept on the wall in her bedroom?

"Well, Grandma Haas is a rabbit, and she can chase the legs off anything, right boy?" she said, and then there was the click of her light switch, and thin beams rose through the open grate in the floor of Joey's room, pushing back the darkness some, just enough, so that finally he could fall into an uneasy sleep.

The next morning, when Joey came down the stairs, he found Grandma Haas at the table, sitting there and looking weary, with dark smears under her eyes, and there was no mention at all of rabbits now, just her veined hands moving and leaping on the tablecloth, chasing down crumbs and specks, as she announced, "He's coming back, so we're going for a walk, to get ready."

Joey was happy, thinking she meant his new step-father, and that meant his mother, and after breakfast he followed her across the lawn, the heavy dew soaking their shoes, to the sidewalk where she surveyed the lilac bushes ready to bloom and pinched the buds with approval.

Sometimes old men in their yards waved hoes and rakes at them, smiling; and old women, wearing shawls like Grandma's, and standing in their screen doors or outside on kitchen chairs as they cleaned their windows with vinegar water, waved their limp rags and called out what a fine morning, what a fine day — "So eina shaynas mordiga, nit?" — didn't they think so too?

Joey would nod at them, and his Grandma would say something about people making the calendar but God making the weather, or that the wind was blowing summer right through town and into their laps, ay, and then they would go on again, walking past the neat clapboard houses and clean lawns, and Joey thought and wondered about those rabbits from the night before, where they'd gone and where they burrowed now in the daylight.

A few minutes later as they were walking along a street that edged an open lot littered with rusting farm equipment, Joey saw an old man in a brimmed hat and dark vest coming at them out of the long weeds, like a dog wading a creek, and calling out greetings to them.

"We crossed the ocean once, this old flower here and me, this bluma," the old man said to Joey, ending close. "From the Black Sea in Russland to this little Stadt in the middle of Nord Dakota — hoi, all the way over those stormy waters together we crossed."

"Crossed? — that's what you think," Grandma said, surveying the man with an imperious air, then waving him away and muttering little sausages of cursewords in German.

The old man, who'd been gathering buds to make camilla tea, held out his palm to show them, but it was too late, for Grandma had taken Joey by the hand and was leading him away, saying, "Build sod houses in the middle of nowhere, burn cow-mischt in the middle of bone-cracking blizzards and watch grasshoppers so thick they eat up your pitchfork handles? No, that's not for us, right Bu? Isn't that right boy?"

Before Joey could say a word or even agree, she started in again.

"And what's he talking, 'crossed'? He's verruckt — crazy. I never went anywhere. If you move around too much you get vergesslich — don't remember yourself," Grandma said. "No, I stayed put."

They were almost home now, and Joey could see she was walking slower, blinking at the high, cloudless sky; grateful for the slackened pace, he kept turning and staring back at a small weathered house they'd passed. It was where he would live with his mother and stepfather when they returned, "Where we'll all live together," his mother had told him, pointing out the house before she'd left, and now the thought of her sent an ache of loneliness through him.

Then they were in her yard again, and Grandma was telling him how everything had to be clean — "Alles muss sauber sei," she said — for it wasn't every day such an important guest came through one's town; and before Joey could ask who, they set to work. Together, from the upstairs to the basement, they scrubbed, swept, polished and dusted. They hung out the throw rugs she'd braided from old clothing and tossed the worn living room carpets over the sagging clothesline, where it was Joey's job to beat them clean with a fan-shaped wire beater.

When he came inside, weary and with his hands hurting, he could hear her voice again, young and strong, and found her doing the one job she wouldn't entrust to him, running the feather duster from an old chicken wing around the oval frame of the Czar's portrait on the wall in her bedroom; and she was talking like she was talking directly to this man with his uniform and medallions and braid, who seemed to be looking right at her with approval.

"You wouldn't know this place anymore," she said. "Everything's changed since the last time you come when I was eina glana madchen, such a little girl — dirt roads covered over, and voices and pictures caught in boxes like herds of devils that you can turn off and on, and people so merkwurdig, so strange, ay, they dung under the same roofs where they sleep, like animals, scheissdreck anyhow. You wouldn't know this place."

For the rest of the day, while the long shadows fell over New Odessa, and far into the evening, they worked. Then, finally, she sent Joey to bed, and he went thankfully, too tired to even worry about his mother.

When he woke that next morning, the curtains were flapping against his bed, and he could smell spaded earth from the gardens and the sweet heavy scent of lilacs that had bloomed during the night; he knew he had overslept.

When he came down the stairs, she was nowhere to be found. In her bedroom, there was just the portrait of the Czar, staring at him. When he called her name down the basement steps, his voice just sounded empty and hollow, among the potato bins and jars of canned vegetables.

"Have you seen my grandmother?" Joey shouted across the garden to the neighbor Alois Zimmerman, who was sitting on his back steps, running a file over the teeth of a handsaw.

"Seen her? Yah, sure," Zimmerman said, waving his file. "Walking that way — uptown."

Just then Hilma Zimmerman, a large woman with swinging breasts, came to the screen door and said, "Mary? Gone? What was she wearing? That taffeta dress of hers?"

"Taffeta?" Alois said, running the file over the sawteeth with a screech. "I don't know taffeta from Truman's underwear ... but the dress was dark blue, glossy. Yah it was taffeta I spose."

"Ach, the Choey," Mrs. Zimmerman said, taking Joey by the hand across the street to where Hilma Fandrach knelt in her garden, cutting the bottom from a coffee can to set over a tomato seedling.

The two old women talked quickly in German, then Mrs. Fandrach called through an open window into her house, and her husband, Otto Fandrach, who'd been janitor at the high school and fallen twice from its roof, came tapping outside with a cane, and all of them, including Alois Zimmerman, who was still carrying his saw and file, started up the street.

"Lilacs, was she carrying lilacs too?" Mrs. Zimmerman asked her husband.

"Sure lilacs," Zimmerman said.

"We better get out there," Fandrach said.

At the rear of the Magpie Cafe, the entourage stopped to get more help. Joey watched Hilma Zimmerman disappear through the back door and then return, followed by Edna Manke, the cook, and John Case and Erno Sayler, two old veterans carrying their coffee cups and talking about their campaigns from the First World War.

"I never got out of boot camp," Case was saying apologetically.

"I did," Old Sayler said, wheezing. "But it cost me a lung in France."

"I got sick, couldn't help that, influenza," Case said.

"Mustard gas, boiling in that trench like Edna's coffee," Sayler said.

"We got bigger things to worry about than your war stories, you two," Edna Manke said. "Remember — you helped us with her a couple years ago."

"One day in the trenches I seen Hitler," Old Sayler said. "Across the way in the German lines ... same crazy eyes and moustache. I could have plugged him and saved the trouble of a second world war."

"Alois says she was carrying lilacs again," Hilma Zimmerman said.

"Lilacs?" Old Case said, looking into his empty coffee cup.

"You got sick from lilacs in boot camp?" Sayler said. "That's not the way you usually tell that story."

"No, Spanish flu, not lilacs," Case said. "It's Mary who got the lilacs."

"Oh, Mary's been gathering lilacs for the Czar again ... why didn't anyone tell me so," Sayler said. "Holy moly, I was wondering what we was doing in the alley when the coffee is inside."

The small collection of people made their way down the alley and when they came to the highway that cut through New Odessa, they stopped for a rest. Edna Manke, still wearing her hairnet and cooking apron, leaned against a cottonwood tree. Mrs. Fandrach still carried that rusting coffee can with its bottom cut out. Fandrach leaned on his cane, while Alois Zimmerman sat on the curb, sharpening his saw. Joey could see they were all solemn and worried, and just as he was going to ask where they were going and where his grandmother was, Fandrach waved his cane, and they started on again, shuffling and limping along the shoulder of the highway.

"You think someone would stop her," Hilma Zimmerman said, looking directly at her husband Alois.

"She can't remember what she did yesterday," he said. "But she'll tell you how many horses pulled that damn carriage sixty years ago, and which way the Czar's moustaches were pointing too."

Then Herbie Rossler, who did odd jobs for a living and drank up his money in his uncle's bar, came driving up on a bicycle, the tires wobbling and his oversize coveralls flapping around his skinny legs.

"Was isch letzt — is the water tower leaking again?" he asked.

After he was told about Grandma Haas, he took

off on his bicycle again, and by the time everyone had passed the high school and Jake Kattei's Shoe Shop, where Kattei came out holding the sole of a shoe in his hand, to join the group, Rossler came driving back out of breath.

"Out there by the New Odessa sign," he said. "Chust standing there like she was keeping the wind from blowing the whole damn town away."

"Don't argue with her," someone said.

"Yah, it didn't work last time," Fandrach said. "And don't anyone say a word about America ... verstehe? She'll just ask why a whole village would cross an ocean and why if we lived in a new land everyone still spoke German and cooked knipfla and made their own sausage."

Off in the distance, just beyond the last line of houses in town, Joey could finally see his new grandmother. She was standing straight and tall, her blue dress set against the white clouds banked along the horizon.

When they came closer Joey could see she was holding a sprig of lilacs and under her arm she had tucked her ancient clasp purse.

"And what are you doing out in this heat?" Fandrach said.

"Come home with me, Mary," Hilma Zimmerman said. "We can eat blachenda ..."

"And drink coffee too," Erno Sayler added.

"Come out of the sun and I fix your shoes for gar nichts — nothing," Kattei said, his unshaven face squirming around the shoenails he held between his lips. "You used up a lot of shoe leather walking out here."

"Tell her about the quilts," Zimmerman whispered

to his wife. "That worked last time."

"Quilts? I don't want to sew no more quilts. I made enough quilts for both of their armies in my life," Grandma said, nodding at Case and Sayler.

"Yah, come and have a little schnappsla with me," Herbie Rossler said, waving a pint bottle and leaning against his bike for support. "Like that time I cut your grass and brought my bottle into your house and you talked about old times, gel?"

"Remember — your first baby was born under that wagon you bought from the Jew Mackovsky ... and how he called you gypsy because of your black hair ... we were heading north to settle the land," Hilma Zimmerman said quietly. "We was young together."

Grandma Haas looked at her, blinking rapidly, and Joey could see her hands leaping and jumping on her dress as she picked lint and brushed.

"Black hair, me? No, you got the wrong person," Grandma said, grabbing her own hair like a rope to show them. "Does this look black?"

"Black as mine," Hilma Zimmerman said. "Black as mine."

Slowly then the people began to drift back into town, one by one; and Joey watched them as they turned and looked over their shoulders and talked to each other in low voices.

"Maybe if we leave her like that one time," Mrs. Fandrach said.

"Sure, she comes back after a while," Kattei added.

"No use wasting my breath," Old Erno Sayler said. "I don't got much anyway."

"The Czar isn't coming," Herbie Rossler blurted, tossing his empty pint bottle into the ditch and starting his bicycle for town.

"Nobody's coming today," he called back.

"Choey, Choey, leave your grandma here," Hilma Zimmerman said, beckoning to him.

Joey didn't understand, just turned and watched Mrs. Zimmerman walk away; watched her disappear in the distance among the white clapboard houses and garages, and saw there was no one else left, except his grandmother, who stood quietly in the hot sun, holding the wilting lilac blossoms.

"Hear that? Hash gehort?" Grandma said. "She called me your grandma — you're a Haas now — part rabbit, verstehe boy?"

With the wind in his ears and his gaze roaming the hills and pastures and fields that stretched to the horizon, Joey took his grandmother's hand and waited with her.